BILL W. ANI

by

Stephen Bergman and Janet Surrey

ISBN 978-0-573-69174-4 Printed in U.S.A. #4186

IMPORTANT BILLING AND CREDIT REQUIREMENTS

All producers of BILL W. AND DR. BOB *must* give credit to the Author of the Play in all programs distributed in connection with performances of the Play, and in all instances in which the title of the Play appears for the purposes of advertising, publicizing or otherwise exploiting the Play and /or a production. The name of the Author *must* appear on a separate line on which no other name appears, immediately following the title and *must* appear in size of type not less than fifty percent of the size of the title type.

All producers *must* display the following disclaimer on all advertisements, posters and programs:

The publication of this work does not imply affiliation with nor approval or endorsement from Alcoholics Anonymous World Services, Inc.

MUSIC NOTE

Producing groups may license an original score of music composed pianist, Ray Kennedy, available on audio tape or sheet music. Contact Ray Kennedy at ray.kennedy@att.net for licensing information. Rates for use are at the composer's discretion.

Grateful acknowledge ment is made for permission to reprint excerpts — as indicated in the NOTES section following the text of the play — from theree publication of Alcoholics Anonymous World Services.

CHARACTERS

BILL W., born November 26, 1895
LOIS, Bill's wife, born in 1891
DR. BOB, born August 8, 1879
ANNE, Dr. Bob's wife, born in 1880
MAN, playing many different roles
WOMAN, playing many different roles

SETTING

Many different places.

The play takes place from September 1925 to July 1935, except for the Prologue and Epilogue, both set in 1939 and 1955.

The play is in two acts.

The stage is bare. Locations (i.e, Akron, Brooklyn etc.) are defined by furnishings in specific stage areas which are illuminated as necessary with the rest of the stage in black. Chairs, bed, props are sufficient to create the reality. Light and dark, sound and silence, create the magic.

Rapid, fluid transitions between scenes is optimal.

A "live" piano is optimal, and can be onstage throughout, providing transition between scenes. Music is mostly from the 20s and 30s. “Japanese Sandman” was Dr. Bob's favorite song, and in addition to being used in Scene 5, can be the theme song for the production.

Dedicated to Bill W. and Dr. Bob
and all their friends

The authors wish to thank Larry Lane, artistic director of the New Repertory Theatre, Newton, Massachusetts, for directing the first staged readings, March 26,28,30,1990; and also thank Rick Lombardo, Producing Artistic director of The New Repertory Theatre, Watertown, Massachusetts, who directed the 2006 production there and the 2007 Off-Broadway production at the New World Stages, New York, which had it's first performance on March 5, 2007.

ACT I

PROLOGUE

(Spot up: standing on one side of the stage, BILL W. Six feet three inches tall, lanky, and with a commanding presence, BILL wears a well-travelled, dark, pin-striped suit, crisp tie, and speaks in a sharp strong voice.)

BILL. My name's Bill W. and I'm an alcoholic. At a time like this, I wish my partner could be here. As you listen to my story, you'll see how, for all those years before we met, it was like he and I were linked by an invisible thread. I'm talking about the man we all called —

(Other spot up: standing, opposite side of stage, DR. BOB. As tall as BILL, and more chunky, DR. BOB is in shirtsleeves and a colorful tie. He speaks in a homey, down-to-earth way.
NOTE: the two men do not look at each other during this scene.)

BOB. — Dr. Bob, alcoholic. Good t'be here sober. I grew up in St. Johnsbury Vermont, 'bout ninety miles from where Bill W. was born and raised. *(Twinkle in his eye, a wry sense of humor.)* Good state to come from, if y'wanna start a program for drunks, Vermont.

BILL. My parents divorced when I was nine, and I was left with grandfather Fayette. One day Gramps says, "Nobody but an Australian can make and throw a boomerang." "Oh yeah? Well I'll be the first American!" I tried and tried — no luck. And then one day I sawed a piece of wood out of the headboard of my bed, whittled it down...Damn thing almost hit the old geezer in the back of the head! *(Pause)* By the age of fifteen I'd made three vows: number one, to be Number One in anything —

BOB. — anything I did was no use — I was forced by Mother to attend church four times a week. I vowed that when I was free, I'd never darken the doors of a church again — a vow I've kept, religiously, for forty-odd years.

BILL. — my second vow was that one day I'd be accepted at the members-only Mount Equinox Resort, where I met my wife Lois, one of the rich summer folk from New York City —

BOB. — in 1898 I left home for Dartmouth College, where I met my Annie, a Wellesley College girl from Illinois. Drink soon cured my shyness —

BILL. — and my final vow was about booze. After a —

BOB. — after a whirlwind courtship lasting seventeen years, I married Annie, 'n set up my surgery in Akron, Ohio. And I said to my wife: "All I want now is to be normal. I want to be a normal surgeon, with a normal family, in normal Akron, Ohio. And on my tombstone I want: 'DEAD'. *(A shrug.)*

Which is normal.

BILL. — Y'see I'd heard what booze had done to my grandfather, seen what it'd done to my father. I vowed it would never happen to me.

BLACKOUT

Scene 1

LOBBY OF A CHEAP HOTEL

(CLERK behind a desk. Roar of motorcycle, arriving, then sound of rain. BILL, age 30, rushes in, wearing wet motorcycle gear, and hurries to the desk. LOIS ENTERS in motorcycle gear, wet with rain, carrying a rolled-up tent, which she dumps on the floor. She is a petite, attractive, and self-possessed "older" woman of 34.)

BILL. Can I use the phone?

CLERK. If y'kin pay for it.

BILL. *(Picks up receiver.)* Where am I?

CLERK. Egypt…Pennsylvania.

BILL. Jesus Christ! *(Into phone.)* Operator, I want to place a call to New York City. Bigelow 7-3434, Mr Frank Shaw, from Bill Wilson. Reverse the charges. *(Hangs up; to LOIS.)* Here's the patch-kit, honey. See if you can fix the rip in the tent.

LOIS. *(Shivering)* Any chance we can stay here?

BILL. *(To CLERK.)* How much is your cheapest room?

CLERK. Two bucks.

BILL. Sorry, Lo.

(CLERK EXITS.)

LOIS. Maybe our big adventure is over. Riding in the sidecar in the rain is not my idea of fun.

BILL. C'mon, this is jazzy!

LOIS. Let's go back to New York.

BILL. We've hit a slight snag, that's all.

LOIS. It's more than that, Bill.

BILL. What's the matter?

LOIS. Last night.

BILL. Yeah?

LOIS. Remember?

BILL. *(Pause; trying to recall, but it was in an alcoholic "blackout", and he has no memory of "last night".)* Remember what?

LOIS. You stood up singing —'The bombs bursting in air!'— put your fist right through the tent, and the rain poured in!

BILL. So *that's* how the tent got ripped?

LOIS. We had a serious talk. *(She waits.)*

BILL. *(He tries again to recall; no luck.)* Okay, okay, what'd I say?

LOIS. You said it'd be the last time —

BILL. Getting me outa New York has worked so far, mostly. From now on — *(Phone. He grabs it on the first ring.)* Frank? We're in Egypt…Pennsylvania! I took a job as a night watchman at the Portland Cement plant. They're making cement for less than a dollar a barrel, way down the line in cost. The stocks dawdling at 15 — I figure it's worth 25 at least—if I were you I'd buy the hell out of it...You what? *(Repeating to LOIS.)* Five thousand shares, and carry me for a hundred more? G.E.went to *what*? Yeah, I predicted it would, sure. A line of credit — *ten grand*?! Actually, we're just a *little* short of cash. Five hundred will do just fine. Tomorrow we'll tune up the motorcycle and head south for American Cyanamid, then down into the Carolinas and Georgia. So long. *(Hangs up.)* Baby, we're not broke anymore! *(Shouts)* Yes! Goddamnit I knew it would work!

(CLERK ENTERS, hearing the commotion.)

BILL. These Wall Street guys never get up off their butts to go and check out these companies! This scientific analysis of mine is gonna revolutionize the whole damn Market! Hotcha! *(He hugs her, dances her around.)* It's 1925, the big train's moving, and we are on board! I'm telling you — both of you — this country can do anything! We're Number One in the world! *(To the CLERK.)* Right? Right?

CLERK. I...I really don't have an opinion about —

BILL. A bottle of your best bubbly!

(CLERK EXITS.)

LOIS. Bill!

BILL. We gotta celebrate!

LOIS. It's not about money —

BILL. Listen. I promise. Starting tomorrow.

LOIS. Promise?

BILL. Sworn on the family Bible — soon as *it* dries out! *(LOIS is hesitant.)* Y'know, even soaking wet you look gorgeous. That first summer, on Emerald Lake, you in your fancy Abercrombie and Fitch skiff, me in my dumpy town rowboat —

LOIS. *(Opening to him.)* — with a blanket for a sail. My dashing young sailor.

BILL. Do you see it, Lo? We *can* make it, I know it!

LOIS. And start our *own* family?

BILL. Yes! We're on our way!

LOIS. We're making a crossing, Willie, together.

(They kiss.)

Scene 2

ONE AREA OF STAGE, AKRON OHIO.
LIVING ROOM OF DR. BOB'S HOUSE.

(Radio playing next to easy chair. ANNE ENTERS. A short, solid, no-nonsense woman of 54, she is putting on a winter coat and hat, and carries a Bible. Turns down the radio.)

ANNE. Are you ready Bob? Bob?

(DR. BOB ENTERS, jingling change in his pocket. Age 54, tall and bulky. Wears a brown suit and a hat, wild tie and matching socks. Goes to the radio, turns it up, picks up a book, and starts to sink into the chair.)

ANNE. *(Turns off radio.)* Robert! *(BOB stops, caught in awkward half-bend to the chair.).* I don't ask much anymore, but you did promise you'd come with me to this meeting. Henrietta's written a special prayer.

BOB. Henrietta Seiberling, Queen of the Goodyear Rubber Sieberlings — the Princess of Neoprene!

ANNE. Bob!

BOB. Henrietta's the only creature in Akron, if not all of Ohio, who can ruin Christmas with religion! The country's in the crapper —

ANNE. Oh Bob!

BOB. — no jobs, no money, families breaking apart, and she keeps getting messages about me from God!

ANNE. Let's go.

BOB. *(Rising, then suddenly clutching his belly, faking pain.)* Oww!

ANNE. Are you all right?

BOB. It's those damn pains in the old breadbasket again. Like a blast furnace down there. Owww!

ANNE. *(Not really believing him.)* Is it the hospital again? Or the sanitariu —?

BOB. No no, not that bad, no.

ANNE. Well, I guess I'll have to stay then, and look after you.

BOB. No need, Annie. You go ahead. I just need to spend the evenin' dousin' m'self down with milk and bicarb pills and I'll be fine. Truth is, I'm a little worried about tomorrow, bein' all thumbs in surgery.

ANNE. How can you still doubt yourself after all these years?

BOB. *(Sinks into sanctuary of the chair.)* I'm like the fella sittin' around the general store, and a farmer comes in and asks if he wants to work the harvest. "What're ya payin'?" the man asks. "Well," says the farmer, "I'm payin' whatever yer worth." "No thanks," says the fella, "I'll be damned if I'll work for that little." *(He chuckles.)*

ANNE. So here we are again. Do I stay, or go?

BOB. You go for both of us. Wonderful institution, that Oxford Group. Heard the other day that Harry Truman and Mae West joined up — a perfect couple! *(Fiddles with the radio.)* I'll just see if I can catch the Friday night fight, maybe do my hour's reading. *(Picks up book.)*

ANNE. What're you reading?

BOB. Oh this? Fella named James.

ANNE. *(Hopefully)* The Bible?

BOB. Philosopher.

ANNE. *(Suddenly deciding.)* All right, Robert. This time I *will* go. Goodnight. *(EXITS)*

BOB. *(Surprised)* Anne?

(She's gone; he searches for a hidden bottle, sinks back down into the chair, starts to guzzle it hungrily.

BOB remains onstage, in dim light, getting drunk in the chair.)

Scene 3

BROOKLYN STAGE LOCATION: BILL W.'S HOUSE. NIGHT. KITCHEN TABLE.

(LOIS, now 43, in bathrobe, sitting at kitchen table, writing in her journal, reading out loud:)

LOIS. "I'm so alone, unable to tell anyone what's really happening. Have I been lax? No, I've tried everything — even a whole week of drinking with him! How I detest myself for that. How can human beings continue to do the things they know will destroy them, them and their whole precious world, and —"

(BILL, now 39, ENTERS, in filthy bathrobe, dragging a mattress and blanket behind him.
He has not had a drink in a day or two and is shaky and on edge, ready to explode.)

BILL. What're you doin' up?

LOIS. Couldn't sleep.

BILL. Nobody in Brooklyn sleeps anymore.

LOIS. Why the mattress?

BILL. Thought it'd be better down here. Writing?

LOIS. My journal. *(Shuts it, rises to leave.)*

BILL. Please, Lo, stay. I dunno what to do.

LOIS. You need to find work.

BILL. Is the Crash my fault? Don't blame me—blame that nitwit Herbert Hoover!

LOIS. The Crash was five years back. You've had offers. Joe Hirschorn called you 'The Einstein of Wall Street.'

BILL. And then he fires me!

LOIS. You can't sell bonds from a jail cell in Canada. Drunk the day mother died? Not there the night I lost our baby? Passed out on the streets of Manhattan? And now — afraid to go out at all?

BILL. If I stayed upstairs another minute…I…I was gonna jump.

LOIS. Why don't you just stop?

BILL. Goddamnit I don't know!

LOIS. The doctor said that if you don't, you'll die within the year.

BILL. You're so cold.

LOIS. Self-defense. *(Turns to leave; gets her purse.)*

BILL. No, no, don't go.

LOIS. *(Thinks to open purse — money is gone.)* Not again. Where's my money?

BILL. Money? That's all you care about now —

LOIS. My whole week's pay! Twenty-one fifty. For the mortgage.

BILL. Twenty-one fifty? I'm sixty thousand in debt!

LOIS. You stole my money!

(BILL screams, violently sweeps books off table toward her, knocking over chair; crumples down on table.
Pause; they face each other.)

LOIS. I was going to wait until morning, but it is morning. I'm not going to protect you anymore. The adoption bureau closed our case. It's over.

BILL. Shit. Wha...What'd they say?

LOIS. *(Looks at him, at the chaos.)* You don't even have the decency to die! *(EXITS)*

(DR. BOB, in dim light, still in chair drinking, taking off his jacket, suspenders etc.
SOUND OF WAITRESS, SINGING, THROUGH INTO NEXT SCENE: "Mademoiselle from Armentiers, parlay-voo...")

Scene 4

A SMALL BAR IN STATEN ISLAND

(WAITRESS young and attractive, wiping table, continuing singing, heavy Brooklyn accent: "— Mademoiselle from Armentiers, parlay-voo, Mademoiselle from Armentiers, she didn't wear any underwear, Inky-dinky parlay-voo ..." MAN WITH A RIFLE, a simple working class fellow, ENTERS, limping. Waitress lends a hand, sits Man down at table.)

WAITRESS. What the hell happened to you?

MAN. The bus collided with a car. It's out of commission.

WAITRESS. I'll be damned. *(Leans closer.)* You hurt?

MAN. Just a little shooken up. *(Perking up.)* Hey — *nice* perfume.

WAITRESS. Thanks. What's 'at thing?

MAN. Flyin' target rifle. I was gonna do some shootin'.

WAITRESS. On Staten Island? Youse jokin' right? Youse pullin' my leg?

MAN. *(Flirting with her.)* I'd like to, but I ain't.

WAITRESS. *(Flirtatiously)*: Y'better watch it!

MAN. Okay I will. *(She laughs.)* Clay pigeons. Fella built a shootin' range out here.

BILL. *(ENTERING, with golf clubs, wearing cap.)*: When's the next bus? I'm trying to get out to the golf course.

WAITRESS. Half-hour anyways. *(Takes out her pad.)* What'll it be fellas?

MAN. A scotch, and a ham and cheese.

WAITRESS. And for you, big boy?

BILL. Half-hour? *(Reluctantly sits down at the table across from MAN.)* Ditto the ham and cheese, and a ginger ale. *(WAITRESS goes to get drinks.)*

MAN. Doncha drink?

BILL. Nope.

MAN. Religious?

BILL. *(Quickly)* Nope, alcoholic.

MAN. *(Startled)* What's 'at?

BILL. Can't drink. *(Ominous)* If I do, it's wet-brain or death, within the year.

MAN. Holy shit!

BILL. Exactly. Been sober a month. My doctor told me it's not a moral failing on my part, it's a disease —

MAN. A disease!?

BILL. Yeah, like, say, tuberculosis.

MAN. *(Scared, edging chair away from BILL.):* My grandmother *died* of tuberculosis.

BILL. Precisely. *(Taps his temple.)* The cure's right in here. Self-knowledge. It's an allergy — one drink makes you crave another one, and another.

MAN. Like hay fever?

BILL. *Hay* fever? *(Shakes head.)* No, not like hay fever, no. *(WAITRESS ENTERS with drinks, sandwiches; BILL fired up, with confidence.)* I'm allergic, you are not. If I were to take that drink, as you so harmlessly are doing right now, it would lead me on a total bender and I'd wind up tonight in the gutter, dead to the world! *(Threatening; in his face.) I'd turn into a monster, a goddamn maniac!*

MAN. Jesus Christ Almighty!

BILL. Exactly. I *know* this, now. Long's I stay away from that first drink, I'm A-okay.

(Happy, patriotic music from the bar.)

MAN. Hey that's right — it's Armistice Day! Say, where was you in the war?

BILL. France and England...Lieutenant colonel...heavy artillery.

MAN. A leader of men!

BILL. You bet I was, and damn good at —

WAITRESS. *(ENTERING, with bourbons and beers.)* Here y'go boys, it's a holiday — and we're celebratin'. Two boilermakers, on the house!

MAN. Great! Sure y'can't have just one? *(BILL shakes head no.)* But it's a holiday.

BILL. Doesn't matter.

MAN. Applies to holidays too? That's a *bitch! (A toast.)* No more wars! *(BILL raises an empty fist; during what follows, sitting close to the man drinking, he's not listening; staring at the drink; MAN talks directly to him.)* During the war I myself was in the Navy, stationed out in Iowa. Now you're probably going to ask me, 'What the hell was the United States Navy doing out in Iowa,' right? Right? *(BILL reaches for the bourbon, downs it, then the beer.)* Hey, what're you doin'?

BILL. Miss? Another round, for me and my friend.

(Lights in bar go to dim. BILL and waitress dimly seen together. In dim light in Akron Dr. BOB, in his chair, drinking, untucking his shirt from his pants, loosening his tie.

LIGHTS UP ON SAME BAR: after hours. WAITRESS, tipsy, blouse unbuttoned — dancing with a drunken disheveled BILL who's "feeling her up". MAN, in a drunken funk, sits caressing his rifle, staring dazedly at them.)

BILL. Hey doll how 'bout we go where we got some privacy?

WAITRESS. How 'bout that yeah.

BILL. Know anywhere?

WAITRESS. I live above. *(Drunkenly points up.)* In the penthouse!

BILL. Like Lady Astor!

(She and BILL laugh crazily; they try to sneak past the MAN.)

MAN. *(Seeing them.)* Hey. My turn. *(Rising)* It's my turn!

BILL. *(Pushing him.)* Sorry, pal, you lost — bye bye!

MAN. You had your turn now it's my turn —

WAITRESS. Boys, hold on —

(She gets caught in a tug-of-war between them, screams and EXITS.)

MAN. My turn!

(Attacks, they fight, BILL goes down, MAN kicks him.)

BLACKOUT

Scene 5

LIGHTS UP ON AKRON LIVING ROOM

(BOB, alone, totally drunk and disheveled — shirt open and shirt-tails flying, tie undone — singing and trying to tap-dance to "Japanese Sandman".)

BOB. "Here's the Japanese Sandman, sneaking in with the dew, Just an old second hand man, buy your old day from you, He will take every sorrow of the day that is through, And he'll give you tomorrow, just to start life anew..." I'm the Japanese Sandman, with a tattoo on my butt — Haha! Tattoos? I'll show ya tattoos! *(Demonstrates real tattoos on his arms.)* From my salad days! See this? This is a lady, a frail *(Kisses her.)*, and this is a snake, the serpent from the Garden of Eden, and this — *(Gestures to tattoo on his butt.)* whazzat? How'd I get 'em? Don't recall, but I was on fire! It was a blazer, a real blazer — haha! *(Tap-dancing, clumsily.)* All I ever wanted was t' have curly hair, to play the piano, and to tap dance, an' I don't, an' I can't, an' I —

(ANNE ENTERS, key in hand, shocked. Turns off radio. Oblivious, BOB keeps dancing.)

ANNE. Go ahead, kill yourself. *(EXITS)*

BOB. *(Freezes; with drunken delight and self-loathing, slowly raising an index finger in the aid.)* Good idea!

Scene 6

BROOKLYN LOCATION

(BILL at same kitchen table, in stained undershirt, head in a blood-stained bandage — in terrible shape. He is writing a letter. Pitcher of booze on table.)

BILL. *(Reading letter out loud; combative tone, dripping with venom.)* "November 25, 1934. Dear President Franklin Delano Roosevelt! I'm an American. I've fought for freedom and in my opinion this New Deal of yours is one of the most ridicu — *(Stops, corrects it.)* — *cockamamey* ideas in the history of civiliza —" *(Knock on the door.)* Shit. *(BILL gets up, groans in pain, hides pitcher.)* Yeah?

(EBBY THATCHER ENTERS. BILL'S age and an old friend, EBBY is the black sheep of a good family, the THATCHERS of Albany. The last time they were together EBBY was a derelict, now he is transformed: well-groomed, neatly dressed in a crisp suit, sober, alert, glowing with confidence and health — he's become an evangelical Christian.)

EBBY. Afternoon, Bill.

BILL. *(Astonished)*: Ebby Thatcher? I don't believe it. You look A-1.

EBBY. *(Appalled at how he looks.)* And how are *you*, friend?

BILL. Pretty good.

EBBY. What happened to your head?

BILL. *(Quickly)* Slipped on the ice. What's it been, five years? Let's celebrate. *(Brings out the pitcher.)* Gin and pineapple juice. Not that I like the pineapple-goddamn juice, but just in case Lois suddenly appears.

EBBY. Where is she?

BILL. Don't know. *(Hands glass to EBBY.)* Have a drink.

EBBY. No thanks. I don't need that stuff anymore.

BILL. What? You're the biggest drinker I know.

EBBY. My friend, something incredible's happened. Can I tell you about it?

BILL. *(Staring at him.)* Maybe. *(Pause)* Maybe not.

EBBY. Remember Rowland? He was worse than me! His father sent him all the way to Switzerland to be treated by Dr. Carl Jung.

BILL. *(Impressed)* Carl Jung?

EBBY. He was at the clinic for a year, but as soon as he left he went out and drank.

BILL. *(A toast.)* Here's to 'im!

EBBY. Jung told him that further therapy would be useless, and that the only thing that could help him was a vital spiritual awakening.

BILL. Oh God!

EBBY. Rowland comes home and joins this Christian organization — *(BILL groans.)* They don't meet in churches, they meet right in people's homes — the Oxford Group. Lotta high-class people —

BILL. Uh, oh. Those little hairs on the back of my neck are standin' up straight —

EBBY. That's how I used to feel too. So one day I find myself in court in Vermont, about to be locked up again —

'alcoholic insanity.' And there, standing next to'me is Rowland! Sober! He asks the judge to turn me over to him, on condition I come down here and live at the Oxford Group house — the Calvary Mission on 23rd? Yesterday I heard about you.

BILL. What'd you hear?

EBBY. That you're in trouble.

BILL. Trouble? Everybody's in trouble.

EBBY. Bill I've been sober since that day in court, two whole months. It's a miracle! *(Takes out a Bible.)* I want to talk to you about prayer.

BILL. Holy shit!

EBBY. I know, I know, but I did what they told me, got down on my knees, and it worked!

BILL. Okay…Okay…Really. How'd you do it?

EBBY. *I* didn't. It was the grace of God.

BILL. Ah you're talkin' ragtime, buddy!

EBBY. *(Takes out a card and reads from it.)* "The age of miracles has returned." "Men are sinners, but men can be changed" — *if* they follow the Four Absolutes — *(Pointedly) especially* "Absolute Humility."

BILL. Lemmie tell y'somethin'. I'm not an atheist, I believe in somethin', okay? My father's father — my namesake — was a fierce drinker. One Sunday morning he takes himself up to the top of Mount Aeolus out in back of th' house, something happens to him up there, he comes back down and never takes another drink, the eight years 'til he dies. So I believe *somethin'* can happen to people, okay? But with preachers, and prayers, and those lit-tle goddamn candles they light for dead people —

EBBY. You're way ahead of where I was. Least you believe in something. *Use what you do believe in, whatever it is. (BILL stares at him, pours himself another drink, and drinks it down.)* Damnit y'big lug, you don't have to believe in God, you just have to admit that *you're not God,* so that something else, outside that stubborn prickly Vermont self 'a yours, can take hold. You want to drink more than you want to live!

BILL. Look. You're not in my world! *(Grabs him by lapels.)* I don't share your belief.

EBBY. Good.

BILL. Good?

EBBY. Rowland didn't believe Jung. I didn't believe Rowland. This thing works in spite of any belief. *(Takes out a card.)*

BILL. Ebby —

EBBY. Here, take this card —

BILL. — you're my best friend on earth —

EBBY. — the Calvary Mission, the address is on the card —

BILL. — too goddamn late buddy, I'm gone.

EBBY. *(Cheerfully)* See you there, brother, see y'there!

(EBBY EXITS; BILL stares at the card, and drains another drink.)

Scene 7

TOWN'S HOSPITAL, NEW YORK

(BILL lies flat in a hospital bed, absolutely still. EBBY sits beside him, hat in hand, like a mourner. Pause. BILL stirs.)

EBBY. Bill? You there? Can you hear me?

(Pause)

BILL. Yeah. *(Coming to, slowly sits up, looks around; pause; groans.)* Ohhh. Shit. This ain't Heaven, is it?

EBBY. It isn't Hell either.

BILL. I'm not so sure. Where's Lois?

EBBY. She'll be back.

BILL. How long I been here?

EBBY. Two days.

BILL. Jesus. What happened?

EBBY. You don't remember anything?

BILL. *(Tries to clear his head.)* I…I was trying to get to your mission. Got off the subway…hit a few bars. Wound up drinkin' with a guy…a *Swede? (Pause)* That's it…What'd I do?

EBBY. The two of you showed up three times that afternoon, looking for me. That night I got you to the meeting, sat you down with the newcomers.

BILL. *(Recalling)* Oh yeah. Stink of booze and sweat, and piss.

EBBY. The preacher called all those saved by Jesus to come up, and before I could stop you, you marched right up and talked about salvation and how you'd given your life to God.

BILL. *(Appalled)* Oh no. I didn't.

EBBY. You did. It was very moving. My friend, you made your surrender to God!

BILL. Didn't work. Been drunk ever since. How many days?

EBBY. Four. Least you made it into Town's Hospital.

BILL. Been here before. Great menu. Castor oil, cold tomatoes...*(With disgust.)* deadly nightshade. Purge and puke. Lemmie alone Ebby. Get outa here.

EBBY. My friend, what do you say we pray together?

BILL. Get the hell outa here!

EBBY. That's the spirit! I'll be praying for you. And I'll be back tomorrow.

(EXITS. Pause.)

BILL. *(Staring around, looking up.)* Goddamnit I've had it! I'll do anything, anything at all. If there's anyone out there, show me! Goddamnit show me!

(Total, pure silence. Subtle shift in light. BILL stops, transfixed, staring.)

BILL. Doctor? Doctor Silkworth? Doctor Silkworth!

SILKWORTH. *(ENTERS; white coat, white hair, examining mirror on head.)*: What, Bill?

BILL. Something...something just happened. Did the lights flash out there?

SILKWORTH. No.

BILL. In here...the room got light — all lit up! And I...I was seized with...I felt...I can't describe it.

SILKWORTH. Keep going.

BILL. *(Scared)* It was...like I was on top of a mountain...and a wind was blowing, hard, but it was strange because it...it blew right through me...a kind of spirit...right through me...strange...the strangest thing. And then...then I heard the words…'You are a free man.'

SILKWORTH. Was it a voice, talking to you?

BILL. No, well, sort of…no, more like a thought.

SILKWORTH. Your own thought?

BILL. Yes.

SILKWORTH. *(Nods)* How tangible was the wind?

BILL. Only in my mind's eye. *(Terrified)* But am I still sane?

SILKWORTH. I believe so.

BILL. What the hell happened?

SILKWORTH. I'm really not sure. But whatever you've got now, Bill, hang onto it. It's better than *what had you*, a few minutes ago.

Scene 8

AKRON STAGE LOCATION; LIVING ROOM; IN VASE ON TABLE, TULIPS OR DAFFODILS.

(ANNE is talking on the phone to Henrietta Sieberling. BOB is pacing, agitated, jingling change in his pocket.)

BOB. Who asked her to come into my life? It's like having the DTs. Every time I turn around, Henrietta Seiberling. When she says "The Divinity," I wanna puke!

ANNE. You'd like to talk with Bob yourself?

BOB. No!

ANNE. Yes, he's a challenge to me and the Divinity too.

BOB. *(Pretending to puke.)* Ahhhh!

ANNE. Bob's come into your life for a purpose? Perhaps. Thanks for calling again, Henrietta. Goodbye. *(Hangs up.)*

BOB. What are you and the poltergeist of the rubber industry cooking up?

ANNE. Henrietta says she has received a guidance from God that you must admit your secret to the group. She's calling a special meeting, for you to give testimony.

BOB. Those meetings don't help. Did everything they said. Read the Scriptures, even tried to pray. Me, pray? Doesn't work. And the worst is, is that I gave in, sacrificed my belief.

ANNE. Your belief?

BOB. My strong belief in non-belief. *(Venomous)* Those evangelicals are gettin' on my nerves — they're always so goddamn happy! Always goin' around sayin' to each other, *(Mimicking, harshly.)* "I'm maximum!" "Are you maximum?" "I'm maximum!"

ANNE. *(A rare burst of anger.)* You've grown so bitter! You're so full of contempt for good people!

BOB. Well thank you, Annie, for casting that first stone. Appreciate it, really.

ANNE. *(He's hit a nerve.)* Yes, well, Lord knows I'm not perfect.

BOB. *(A look; a beat.)* Why doesn't she work on her own family? There she is, living down in the gatehouse with the kids, and just up the driveway, her husband's holed up in the mansion, alert for her attack!

ANNE. She's a remarkable woman. All these years, I don't know how I'd've managed without her. But you have not done everything she's asked, Bob.Whenever you do come to a meeting, you never reveal your drinking. It's time.

BOB. If word gets out 'n spreads around Akron I'll lose my practice and we're through.

ANNE. People know.

BOB. Nobody's ever said anything to me.

ANNE. Believe me, they know.

BOB. Ah, you don't know what you're talkin' about.

ANNE. The Book of James says, "Faith without works is dead."

BOB. Whatever's wrong with me, it ain't gonna be cured by God.

ANNE. How will it?

BOB. *(Exploding)* Maybe it won't. Maybe this is it, 'n we all better learn to live with it! And not for that much longer either. Y'think that tattooed dancer is bad, wait 'n see what shows up without any drink in me at all. *(A confession.)* I got a demon inside me, Annie, a real live evil spirit called John Barleycorn! Can you understand that? That I gotta have it? Can you?

ANNE. No I cannot.

BOB. And thank Heaven you can't. Stop trying to save me. *(Turns to walk out.)*

ANNE. Robert. *(He stops.)* Next month, it'll be twenty years since you carried me over that threshold into this house. Twenty years. Same threshold, same house. The children have never known you, really, like you were then. That first day, we pitched in, together. Didn't even take a honeymoon — we wanted to get to work, together. I used to think we'd get around to a honeymoon, sometime or other, but no more. There will never be a honeymoon, Bob, never. We've grown old. It's a cruel thing, Bob, a cruel cruel thing.

BOB. All right goddamnit, I'll go! I'll go and I'll talk! *(Pause; at door.)* Happy?

Scene 9

NEW YORK

(LOIS and EBBY at BILL'S house, same kitchen table and chairs, EBBY sitting, LOIS placing meagre dinner on table. BILL was due some time ago.)

LOIS. *(Irritated)* We've waited long enough. Let's start dinner without him.

EBBY. It's a miracle. Bill hasn't had a drink in four months and eighteen days.

LOIS. *(Puts casserole on table, sits.)* Here. It's beans again. *Mainly.*

EBBY. Bill's always been a phenomenon. When he speaks at the mission, he draws people to him.

LOIS. Some phenomenon. I've gone from supporting one grown man to supporting two.

EBBY. Oh…Well, um…I can always move back to the mission.

LOIS. It may just come to that.

EBBY. By the way could I bother you for some butter?

LOIS. Butter? *(A look; gets up, gets butter, stands there with butter dish; sarcastic.)* Look…it's just that, if it were remotely possible, without cutting into your charity work in the least, to take a job? *One* of you? To work? For *money?*

EBBY. Who would've thought you or I would ever have to worry about money?

LOIS. Those days are gone.

EBBY. You've really held things together haven't you. I knew you had it in you — that summer at the resort you were what? Twelve? Thirteen? — you surprised us all and set up that little tea house on the island, I said to myself, 'That girl will —'

LOIS. — will wind up selling blouses at Loesser's! Not at all what I had in mind, without children.

EBBY. Yes, yes, I understand how hard it is.

LOIS. Do you? He hasn't been drinking, but is *this* better? It's like he's on a crusade.

EBBY. We've just got to make sure to keep our faith and hold on.

LOIS. "We"? *I'm* holding onto my job, but what exactly are *we* holding onto, eh?

EBBY. Lois, you're a miracle!

LOIS. *(Fed up.)* Is there anything that's *not* a miracle to you these days?!

(BILL rushes in, transformed. Wearing a dark, well-worn pin-striped suit and tie, he is well-groomed and bursting with manic energy, high as a kite, talking fast. Carries a bunch of tulips or daffodils.)

BILL. Sorry I'm late. Let's eat! What a day! Ran into a fella I've been workin' on for a month — he went out on a bender and I chased him all the way up to the Bronx! Talked to him for an hour! He may come to the mission, Ebby, *he may come!*

EBBY. Great Bill, just —

BILL. And on the way back down I stopped in to consult with Doc Silkworth. Found some flowers, Lo, for you.

LOIS. *(Icy tone.)* Put them in the sink. *(He doesn't; she gets up to do so.)* Sit down.

BILL. *(Not sitting; to EBBY.)* But get this — he tells me I'm on a twin-engine power drive, one part genuine spirituality, one part my old drive to be the Number One Man. Says my problem is I'm preachin' to 'em, drivin' 'em away, and that I oughta just keep talkin' about my illness? So I dunno, Ebby —

LOIS. We've been waiting for you.

BILL. *(Not attending to her.)* — y'think he's got something there? Y'think so, Eb?

LOIS. *Sit down! (She stands there.)*

BILL. Right, right. *(He sits, but keeps on talking to EBBY.)* But the good doctor just can't see the energy of this thing, the way it's gonna take off. For five thousand years the batting average with drunks has been zero. *Everybody's* given it a shot — Women's Temperance, FDR — and everybody's failed! I'm going to cut down to what really works. *I'm* gonna start a chain reaction that'll reach *all the drunks in the world!*

(Pause. LOIS and EBBY look at each other.)

LOIS. Well Ebby, how's that for "absolute humility"?

EBBY. Hmm. Seemed a bit more humble than usual.

LOIS. Bill, eat. *(She moves away.)*

BILL. *(Puts food on his fork, but leaves it suspended in mid-air.)* I must'a talked to twenty alcoholics today — and I think I got a new one — get this, a woman. My first woman drunk! Y'believe it?

LOIS. *(Coming back to the table, standing there; an old wound.)* A woman?

BILL. Yeah. I was with her for two hours, and I almost got through to her.

LOIS. How pretty was she, Bill?

BILL. Hey, I'm *working*, understand? Nothing happened, okay?

LOIS. Two whole hours, and nothing? Then how come you're so jazzed?

(Pause.)

BILL. *(Containing his own anger, staring at the stuff on his fork, and then down at his plate.)* What *is* this?

LOIS. Bean casserole. *Over-done.* All we can afford. You've got to find a job.

BILL. I *have*! *(Pause)* I've been waiting for the right time, to surprise you. I'm investigating a tire company for a takeover. I leave in two days for Akron.

LOIS. Akron?

EBBY. *Ohio?* You're not ready to go to Ohio — in your condition —

BILL. My condition?

EBBY. None of us are on solid ground yet, Bill.

BILL. I checked it out with Silkworth. He says okay — it's not for long.

LOIS. You mean it's not a permanent job? All the way to —

BILL. *(Exasperated)* Isn't this what you wanted? *(A stare from her.)* It could be something really big. They say if it works I could come back as president of the company!

LOIS. Oh, Bill!

(LOIS shakes her head, turns her back on him. BILL tries to eat.)

EBBY. *(Trying to change the subject.)* Y'know, Bill, the Group's getting' kinda nervous, all the drunks you've been bringin' in.

BILL. Tell me about it.

EBBY. Last night one of 'em threw his shoe through the stained glass window of the church!

BILL. Look. Truth is, they don't want to deal with my drunks — they think they're too low class, or not trying hard enough to get the "moral principles." *(Sharply, to EBBY.)* Hell, the *last* thing a drunk wants is a moral principle. I dunno, maybe Silkworth's right — talk to a drunk about God, next thing you know you're chasin''im through the Bronx!

EBBY. *(Irritated by this, gives him a look, then gets up.)* Yeah well it's a beautiful evening, I think I'll go to the Promenade. Thanks, Lo.

(A look at BILL. EBBY EXITS. Pause.)

BILL. *(Discouraged)* I'm getting' the shit beat outa me on all sides. *(Really down.)* After all this, *I'm* battin' zero — none of 'em are stayin' sober. Maybe it's all just a great big goddamn waste of time.

(Pause.)

LOIS. *(Suddenly feeling more for him.)* Well, Bill, all your talking to alcoholics is working for at least *one* of them.

BILL. Who's that?

LOIS. *(Reaches out her hand and touches his cheek tenderly.)* You.

BLACKOUT

(Sound of group — from next scene ANNE, HENRIETTA, T. HENRY singing: Amazing Grace: "Amazing Grace, how sweet the sound...")

Scene 10

OXFORD GROUP MEETING IN A HOME IN AKRON

(BOB, ANNE, HENRIETTA and T. HENRY WILLIAMS moustache, glasses, etc. are sitting in a semicircle, finishing singing "Amazing Grace." BOB not singing, The rest of the group — ten others — are unseen.)

HENRIETTA. I feel such gratitude to T. Henry and Clarace for opening your beautiful home to us for these meetings. Do you wish to give testimony now, T. Henry?

T. HENRY. Thank you, Henrietta. Ahem. Now I'd have to say my main shortcomin' today is the way, despite all my willpower and my prayer, I can't seem to stay away from that gol-darned self-centerednesss. *(A cough.)*. And tune in to my direct access to that Power which is the Living God. Ahem. Now, I'd have to say that absolute honesty and absolute purity ain't too tough for me. *(A sniff.)* But that there absolute love's a real twister! Clarace and I sit every mornin' in silence for a half hour, seekin' guidance. Every so often there's a small victory, at home with the little whippersnappers. Or in the tire factory. Ahem. That's it. *(He smiles.)* I'm *maximum. (BOB grimaces.)* Thank you. Henrietta?

HENRIETTA. Thank you T. Henry. I'm sure we *all* can identify with what you said.

(HENRIETTA looks at ANNE, then both — and T. Henry — look at BOB, who is startled. BOB feels the pressure. Pause.)

BOB. Well, you good people have all shared things that I'm sure were very costly to you, and so I reckon I'm goin' to tell you somethin' that may cost me my profession here in Akron. *(Pause)* I'm a secret drinker, and I can't stop. I've sworn on the Bible a hundred times that I'd quit tomorra. Each time, I mean it, and it doesn't work. I've been in the sanitariums a dozen times — more. The price to Anne and the kids is tremendous. I know it, and still, I can't stop.

HENRIETTA. Do you want us to pray for you?

BOB. *(Not sure, but says it anyway.)* Yes.

(All but BOB bow heads in silent prayer.)

Scene 11

LOBBY OF MAYFLOWER HOTEL AKRON.
SATURDAY AFTERNOON.

(One side: entrance to bar — music, laughter. Other side: propped up on a stand, a 'Church Directory'. BILL ENTERS, in great agitation. He is stranded alone in a strange hotel. Drawn toward the bar, he takes a few steps, and then stops, in agony. Looks around, spots the Church Directory, and immediately goes to it. Picks a name out of the fifty or so; picks up phone.)

BILL. Operator, get me Poland 868.

(Rings; spot up, to one side, REVEREND TUNKS picks up phone.)

TUNKS. Hello?

BILL. Hello, is this the Reverend Walter F.Tunks?

TUNKS. Speaking.

BILL. *(Absolutely desperate.)* My name's Bill Wilson, I'm a stockbroker from New York, I'm in the lobby of the Mayflower Hotel and *I need help!*

TUNKS. How can *we* help?

BILL. *(Talking fast.)* I've been in Akron a week working on a business deal. Yesterday the thing fell through my partners went back to New York leaving me t'pick up the pieces — it's a colossal disappointment! I'm a drinker'n I keep being pulled toward the bar — I need to talk to another *drunk.* So I went to the Church Directory and picked out *your* name.

TUNKS. You think *I'm* a drunk?!

BILL. No no I thought you could give me the name of a drunk — I'm not crazy.

TUNKS. Do you want us to pray with you?

BILL. Tried it. Didn't work.

TUNKS. Tell me, how did you choose to call us?

BILL. I don't know.

TUNKS. Was it because we're Episcopalian? Are you Episcopal?

BILL. No, alcoholic!

TUNKS. Right. Got a pencil? I'll give you some names. These people may be able to help.

(BILL starts to write. Spot down on TUNKS. Lights on BILL dim briefly, then back up. Note: not in real time here.)

BILL. *(Picks up phone.)* Operator? Get me Poland 527.

(Rings; WOMAN, young, frantic, baby on shoulder, rushes to phone, in spot.)

WOMAN. Johnson residence.
BILL. I'm looking for Stretch Johnson?
WOMAN. *(Angry)* Well so'm I! If you find him, tell him to call! *(Hangs up, spot out.)*
BILL. Operator? 281? *(Rings; drunken MAN staggers into spot.)*
MAN. Hello?
BILL. Is Frank Sullivan there?
MAN. Yeah, I'm him
BILL. My name's Bill, I'm an alcoholic from New York, and —
MAN. Ah you go to hell! *(Slams phone down; spot out.)*
BILL. SAME TO YOU PAL! SHIT! *(Sighs)* Operator. 244.

(Lights dim on BILL briefly. Music, happy bar sounds swell. He takes off his jacket. Lights up on BILL. This is his tenth call.)

BILL. Operator? 648?

(Rings; in spot, NORMAN SHEPARD, putting on his coat and hat, in a rush to catch a train.)

NORMAN. Hello?

BILL. Norman Shepard?

NORMAN. Yes?

BILL. *(Really desperate now, a matter of life and death.)* I'm Bill Wilson I got your number from Reverend Tunks. I'm from New York, and, well, this is going to sound very strange, Norman?

NORMAN. *(Looking at his watch, needing to leave.)* Yeah?

BILL. I've been on the wagon five months I'm about to slip off and that would be *suicide!*

NORMAN. I'm sure it would, Mr. Wilson, but how can *I* help?

BILL. You're not a *drinker*, are you?

NORMAN. Sorry, no.

BILL. Can you put me in touch with one?

NORMAN. Not now, I'm just catchin' the Zephyr for New York myself. *(BILL groans in disappointment.)* Did the Reverend Tunks give you any other names to call?

BILL. He gave me ten *and you're the tenth*! Aren't there *any* drunks in Akron?!

NORMAN. Hey wait. You call Henrietta Seiberling, she's in some organization called Oxford something or other. Very religious.

BILL. Any relation to Frank Seiberling, the president of Goodyear? I've met him. I could never call his wife.

NORMAN. Not his wife, his daughter-in-law. She's at 522. *(Firmly) You call her. (Hangs up, spot out; BILL calls immediately.)*

BILL. 522!

(Spot up, HENRIETTA SEIBERLING.)

HENRI. Hello?

BILL. Henrietta Seiberling?

HENRI. This is she, yes.

BILL. My name's Bill, I'm from the Oxford Group, and I'm a rum-hound from New York. I'm at the Mayflower Hotel, I'm sober five months, but I'm —

HENRI. Good for you!

BILL. Thanks. But I'm staring at the bar and it looks mighty appealing and the only thing that'll stop me is to talk to another drinking man.

HENRI. *(Overwhelmed, covers phone.)* Oh my. This really is manna from Heaven!

BILL. Hello? Hello? Don't hang up please!

HENRI. I'm right here, Bill. I know just the man! You march down that main staircase, hail a cab, and come right out here. Tell the taxi to bring you to Stan Hywet *('Hew-it')* Hall.

BILL. *(A little stunned by it all.)* Stan Hywet? What's that?

HENRIETTA. Why it's Welsh, for 'Rock Is Found Here.'

BILL. *(Smiling, 'going with the flow" of these strange things.)* Looks like I'm on my way! (EXITS)

(Immediately HENRIETTA dials. Lights up on empty Akron living room. Sound of BOB singing offstage: "happy mother's day to yooo —")

ANNE. *(ENTERING, looking back at offstage Bob, picks up phone.)*: Hello?

BOB. *(Offstage, approaching, singing drunkenly:)* "Habby Mother's Day tooo yooo…"

HENRI. Hello Anne, it's Henrietta. You and Bob must come over immediately, to meet a friend of mine, a sober drinking man named Bill.

BOB. *(ENTERING, terribly drunk, wobbling under a large potted plant he is carrying in his arms, singing.)* "Habby Mother's Day too yooo…." *(He tries to give it to her.)*

ANNE. *(Turns back on BOB, tries to shoo him off. Into phone:)* I'm not sure this is the time.

BOB. *(Following her with the plant.)* "Habby Mother's Day too yooo…"

ANNE. *(Covers the receiver.)* Bob? Bob! Stop!

BOB. *(Standing up on a chair, wobbling precariously.)* "Habby—"

ANNE. Go back! Go back out, at once!

BOB. "— Mother's Day too yooo…"

ANNE. Mother's Day is *tomorrow*!

(BOB falls off chair, lies face down on floor, dead still. ANNE stares; ominous pause.)

HENRI. Anne? Are you there Anne?

BOB. *(Singing)* "Habby Mother's Day tooo yooo…" *(Continues to sing softly.)*

ANNE. I'm afraid he's too drunk to drive.

HENRI. Well then you must drive him.

ANNE. He's incoherent.

HENRI. Oh. Well *how* incoherent is he?

BOB. "— Habby Mother's Day love you honey habby day."

ANNE. Totally. He shan't be in any shape until late tomorrow, at best.

HENRI. I see. Well then, bring him tomorrow, at five.

ANNE. *I'll try. (Slams the phone down.)* Bob? ROBERT! *(He stops singing.)* You are a contemptible man! You are never again going to humiliate me in front of my friends — or my children! You're no doctor, you haven't been a husband or a father for years, you're a...a weak, pathetic sot! *(EXITS)*

(BOB, stung to the core, makes a feeble gesture toward her, but she's gone.)

Scene 12

THE NEXT AFTERNOON AT FIVE. HENRIETTA'S GATEHOUSE ON THE STAN HYWET ESTATE.

(BILL and HENRIETTA greeting BOB and ANNE. BOB is terribly hungover from day before, feeling like hell, with a bad case of the "shakes". He is hunched in on himself physically, restless and resentful.)

HENRI. Bill Wilson, meet Dr. Bob Smith and his wife Anne.

ANNE. Pleased to meet you —

BOB. *(Gruffly)* 'fraid we can only stay about fifteen minutes. Fifteen minutes, *tops.*

BILL. Looks like you could use a *drink.* *(HENRI and ANNE are shocked.)*

BOB. *(Licking lips, interested.)* Yeah, maybe I could.

(Awkward pause.)

HENRI. *(Trying to save the situation.)* Yes…well. *Grand!* Now, since time is so short, why don't you two talk. I shall make some *coffee.*

BILL. Sounds good to me. Bob?

(BOB grunts his assent.)

HENRI. Anne?

(She nods; ANNE and HENRIETTA EXIT.
Pause. BOB stands apart, clutching himself, shaking badly, feeling like crap. BILL pulls up a chair, so there are two chairs facing each other downstage center.)

BILL. Thanks for coming. You're probably wondering what the hell's going on, Henrietta dragging you over here to listen to me.

BOB. *(Pause)* Uh hunh.

BILL. Where you from?

BOB. *(Pause, reluctantly.)* Vermont.

BILL. Say I'm from Vermont too.

(No response from BOB.)

BILL. What town?

BOB. *(Reluctantly)* Saint Johnsbury.

BILL. Still got that trucking outfit up there?

BOB. Wouldn't know.

BILL. I'm from East Dorset. Small village outside —

BOB. Manchester. Vermont, eh? Well that's quite a coincidence.

BILL. *(A beat.)* I'm a real nasty drunk, sober five months and one day, today. Last night I was knocking around the Mayflower Hotel, alone, about to take a drink. *(Checks watch.)* We got twelve minutes. I'll give you the Reader's Digest version: condensed. Y'game?

BOB. *(Shaking, goes to chair, sits; uses a hand to pull one leg up across the other; sarcastically.)*: Fire away.

BILL. Okay. Where to begin? In 1918, waiting to go off to war, I'm bivouacked at New Bedford. Massachusetts. The rich families insist on entertaining us soldiers. I sit at these formal dinners, could hardly speak. Well one night a pretty girl hands me a Bronx cocktail, and I took my first drink, and another, and then — it's a miracle! The strange barrier between me and all men and women seems instantly to go down! I feel I *belong* to life, hell, to the universe! That first night, I get plastered—pass out in fact. Doc, the story that followed takes me from the highest peak of the financial game right down to the gutter. I flunk out of law school, fly an airplane drunk from Albany to Manchester, hiding booze, stealing from my wife, lies, jails, hospitals —

BOB. How *old* are ya?

BILL. Thirty-nine.

BOB. I'm fifty-five. Got sixteen years on ya. Keep firin'.

BILL. I ended up in the hospital. My doctor told me that he believes that alcoholic allergy is a disease, and so I figure—

BOB. *(Astonished)* A medical disease?

BILL. Yeah.

BOB. *(Stunned)* A disease? *(As a doctor, analyzing it.)* With signs and symptoms, a course and a progression? What, implying what? — a treatment?

BILL. Makes sense, does it, I mean medically?

BOB. Yes. Yes, it does. Why couldn't *I* see that?

BILL. Most doctors can't. (pause) So I figure: this is it — self-knowledge right? Didn't work. The next piece of the puzzle is, well…*(He hesitates to use the word.)* call it 'spiritual.' *(BOB lets out a long extended groan.)* One afternoon an old buddy, a hard drinker named Ebby, shows up — sober — with a message for me from Dr. Carl Jung. Ebby'd joined the Oxford Group and —

BOB. Oxford. Wife'n I been goin' to those damn meetin's for years.

BILL. *(Notes the coincidence.)* Ebby tells me its' not about willpower — you could have all the willpower in the world and it wouldn't be enough. He said I had to make a surrender to God, or to whatever I could —

BOB. Oh pleeese!

BILL. I know I know! I'd gotten pretty cynical about things like that, but I tried it. Went to meetings, but I was still getting loaded. One day back in the hospital, I hit rock-bottom, and well…something *else* happened to me. But in the interest of time —

BOB. No, no, go on.

BILL. Let's just say I had a kind of 'flash,' and I haven't had a drink since.

BOB. *(Impressed)* You…you talkin' about something like…a 'conversion experience'?

BILL. *(Delighted)* You've read William James!

(BOB reaches into his pocket, takes out a worn wallet, searches in it for a frayed, folded piece of paper. Hands shaking, he opens it up, and reads.)

BOB. "The sway of alcohol over mankind is unquestionably due to its power to stimulate the mystical faculties of human nature, usually crushed to earth by the cold facts and dry criticisms of the sober hour." *(Folds it back up, replaces it in wallet.)* Buddy, I've read everything I thought might help. Even read that crazy sonofabitch Freud. For a *long* time he loused me up, tellin' me it was all in my toilet training! *(BILL laughs; BOB smiles.)* Keep talkin'.

BILL. So then what'd I do? Tried to convert all the drunks in New York City! And how many did I get? None. Not one. All this time something's been missing. In that hotel lobby yesterday, I knew — preachers, doctors, my wife, my friends — none of 'em could help me.

BOB. Yeah, why not?

BILL. *'Cause they're not drunks!* They don't know what it's like to wake up, your head bloody and a golf bag in your arms and a woman standing over you who maybe is your wife — and maybe not — and the veins in your temples pounding on bone. They don't know what it's like, every cell in your body dry as sand, thirsting for the one thing in the world you know will destroy you —

BOB. *I* do.

BILL. *(Pulls up chair, back facing BOB, sits with arms crossed over back of chair.)* Now I don't want to get too far out here, Bob — we're both men of the world, rational men who've lived through a great war, sensible men — but maybe there's a reason I'm sittin' here. In that hotel lobby, I *knew* — knew in my guts like a man knows he's gonna die — that to stay out of that bar I needed help. And then I realized that what I needed was another drunk to talk to, just as much as he needed me. Friend, I need your help.

BOB. *(Puzzled)* Um…how can *I* help?

BILL. *(Considering)* I think you just have. *(Checks his watch.)* We're out of time. *(Rises, offers his hand.)* Thanks.

BOB. *(Still seated.)* What's yer rush? We can take a little more time.

BILL. Okay. *(Sits back down; waits; BOB says nothing; waits.)* I…I'm listening.

BOB. *(Appalled at what he's gotten himself into; a loud groan.)* Ohhhhh. *(Pause)* Well, uh…um…I dunno…what you said — with no horse manure thrown in — it's like listenin' to myself. *(BILL nods — throughout this he's listening intently.)* I did all that — *all* of it — flunked outa med school — twice! — my father the Judge comin' all the way out to Chicago with the town doctor, the two of 'em draggin' me home to Vermont. *(Ashamed)* I chose medicine 'cause of that wonderful old doc. Last person on earth I'd want to disappoint. I was thirty-two when I finally got my degree, took me seventeen years to marry Annie — my whole life's been slowed down. You've lived three lives, Bill, I've barely lived one. You've heard the expression 'When Hell freezes over'?

BILL. Sure have.

BOB. I'm barely movin' anymore. *(Pause)* I use pills and booze every day. I wake up with the jitters, take a sedative to steady my hands for surgery, start drinkin' again in the afternoon, needin' to get drunk to sleep. I'm *terrified* of not bein' able to sleep. Sometimes, in the operating room, I'm high as a kite. Lucky I haven't killed somebody. *(Sighs; brightening, with a wink.)* Prohibition was murder, wasn't it?

BILL. Worst thing you can do to a drunk is pass a law to try'n stop him. He gets *very* serious about it, then.

BOB. Oh yeah. *(They laugh; pause.)*

BOB. Bill, I tried my best to believe, but I can't. I've sworn off God. The lid's on tight.

BILL. *(Realizing it for the first time.)* Maybe we'd just better leave God out of it for now. I want to hear about you and booze.

BOB. *(Inching his chair closer.)* If I don't drink, I'm a monster. Booze is the glue holdin' me together, the one thing I can count on. And now the goddamn stuff doesn't even work anymore — with or without it, I'm a monster.

BILL. The monster is our disease.

BOB. You really *believe* that, Bill?

(BILL nods; BOB is overwhelmed by this, the sense that here at last is a person who understands what he's gone through from his own experience. Tears come to his eyes.)

BOB. Christ. I always figgered a drunk was a bum under a bridge, not folks like us. Here I am, a physician, and I got to wishin' *I* could be that bum, under that bridge. But you're sayin' that what I needed all along was to come clean to one hard-core, nose-in-the-gutter drunk?

BILL. *(Opening his arms to him.)* You found him, Bob. 'Fire away!'

BOB. Right. *(Inching his chair closer.)* I left home for

Dartmouth College in eighteen hundred and ninety-eight. I'll never forget that feelin' — finally, I was free! See, I always dreamed of bein' able to tap-dance, play the piano, and have curly hair — and when I was loaded, I did tap-dance, and played the piano, and Christ, for all I knew, I did have curly hair, and...

(Note: Light now is a glowing gold spot in the dark. *The men sit on the edges of their chairs, leaning over and in toward each other, absorbed in talking and listening, attending and responding. Their hands and faces reveal the intensity of their shared energy. The "feel" is of a tremendous sense of peace.*

Lights dim. BILL gets up and gets two cups of coffee, brings them back. Lights up. BILL and BOB now have their jackets off, ties loosened, sleeves rolled up, talking animatedly. Light is brighter, crisper — the "feel" is of fresh, new energy, unleashed, filling the words and actions of both men.)

BOB. *(Shouting back at HENRIETTA offstage, irritated at being interrupted.)* Okay, okay, Henrietta! We know it's been six hours! Really we'll be right there! *(To BILL, with real zest, a changed man.)* But we've had people tryin' to tell us what's wrong with us all our lives — it just gets our backs up, makes us dig in our heels. They can't fix us, with that.

BILL. *(Revved up.)* No, Smithy, they can't. But telling our own stories, to each other...yeah, being honest about it — about who we are and what happened to us, well, that's real, and has the ring of truth to it, and maybe when we're tellin' it, something true makes its way across the gap between one drunk and another, like sound waves or light rays, and maybe, when no one's lookin', it slips in under the ribs and hits the other fella's heart!

BOB. Yeah, but you're gettin' kinda complicated about it, *Abercrombie*, I mean you're puttin' in a lotta fireworks and magic, and —

BILL. Look — I can see the shape of the whole thing emerging!

BOB. Well if this new treatment a'yours works, we've got no choice but to try it on others.

BILL. *(Realizing that BOB has joined him.)* We? *(BOB nods.)* Don't worry — I'll go easy on the fireworks. Hell, maybe the main thing about that flash of mine was just to move me along to this meeting with you. If there's any miracle, partner, this is it!

BOB. *(Getting up.)* Yeah, well, I dunno about things like that. *(Twinkle in his eye; a small victory.)* But it looks like it's not religion after all. It's just other drunks — 'n maybe somethin' else workin' through us.

BILL. We'll save hundred, thousands, millions!

BOB. Let's just get one more.

END OF ACT ONE

ACT II

Scene 13

(Roar of a big fast train — The Twentieth Century — hissing to a stop. Akron, BOB'S house. Four in the morning. ANNE, in bathrobe, at kitchen table, waiting anxiously.

BOB, unable to walk and supported by BILL, staggers into the kitchen of his house, groaning and shaking. He is on the verge of the DTs.)

ANNE. *(Rising from chair, shocked.):* Oh my God.

BILL. He's worse than I thought. Gimmie a hand.

ANNE. Oh dear God!

(With great effort they manage to dump him into his chair. He sits, groaning, holding his head, shading his eyes from the light.)

BOB. A drink fer Chrissakesakes a drink.

ANNE. I told you this would happen! How could you do this to us?

BOB. A drink!

BILL. Right. I'll get you a hooker of scotch. *(Takes bottle and glass from sideboard.)*

ANNE. *(Snatching bottle from him.)* What? Are you crazy?

BILL. He needs it.

BOB. I need it! *(Lunging at bottle, falling down on floor, crawling toward it.)* A drink!

ANNE. Haven't you had *enough*? *(To BILL.)* More alcohol? Are you mad?

BILL. The man's about to have a seizure! It's dangerous —

ANNE. Not in my house! I agreed to let you live with us — but keeping bottles right out in the open? "Bob has to learn to live with temptation" — what a hair-brained idea that was!

BILL. A seizure could kill him.

BOB. For Chrissakes a drink!

ANNE. I'm throwing this out!

BOB. Noooo!

BILL. He's got the shakes bad! Please — we've got to bring him down gradually —

BOB. Pleeeze!

ANNE. *(Not giving up the bottle.)* I *knew* it was absurd to let a man, just two weeks sober, go off to the Medical Convention. All the way to New Jersey? For five days? With other *doctors? (To BILL.)* Whyever did I listen to you?

BILL. Okay I was wrong, but —

ANNE. You said this thing was working, and this may be as bad as I've ever seen him!

BILL. I made a mistake, but he needs —

ANNE. *I* know what he needs. He needs another trip to the sanatarium!

BOB. No! *(A bit clearer.)* I g…gotta op…operate Mon… Monday mornin' at nine!

ANNE. *(Staring at him as if he's insane.)* What?!

BILL. *(Considering this.)* Okay. That gives us three whole days.

ANNE. Three days? It'll take three *weeks* to dry him out. *(BILL moves to sideboard to get Mason jar of tomatoes, and Karo syrup.)* C'mon, help me get him back into the car. *(ANNE tries to lift him to his feet.)* Bob? *(BOB is staring at the bottle.) Bob!*

BOB. *(Holds his head.)* Shhh! Whisper.

ANNE. Get up. We're taking you in. Bill?

BOB. *(Trying to clear his head.)* If I don't show up Monday I'm…

ANNE. Impossible.

BILL. Maybe not. Let me take care of him. I'll use the Town's treatment.

ANNE. *(Stares at him, and shakes her head.)* After all you've done, you have the nerve to talk about *another* "treatment"?

BILL. *(Nodding with shame.)* I know, I know. But I've been through it myself, a lot of times. *(To BOB.)* We'll build you up with Karo corn syrup for energy, cold tomatoes for vitamins, and taper you off with…well… *(Glance at ANNE.)* alcohol and sedatives. *(A look from ANNE.)* We've got to bring him down gradually, and all we've got is booze and his stash of pills.

ANNE. I should trust you *again?*

BOB. *(Rallying, sitting up, begging her.)* Let him try Annie. *(Pause; she stares at him.)* I'm beggin' you. Let him and me try.

(Pause. ANNE stares at them. She realizes that BOB has a shred of faith left — in BILL.)

ANNE. Bill, you're a man who could talk a dog off a meat wagon. *(Puts the bottle down on the table; BOB snatches at it; BILL takes a glass, measures it out, hands it to him; with a yelp BOB drinks it down hungrily and gestures for another.)* It's four in the morning. I'll give you 'til four tomorrow afternoon. Put him in the spare bed in your room. And don't wake the children. *(EXITS)*

BILL. *(Gives BOB another drink.)* Here you go, Smithy. *(Gulps it down, asks for another, BILL stops him.)* Now. Where do you keep your sedatives?

BOB. *(Foggy)* Sedatives?

BILL. Your supply of goofballs? *(Louder, emphasizing.)* The pills you told me —

BOB. Shhh! *(Holds head.)* Can't remember. Las' thing I 'member was boardin' *The Twentieth Century.*

BILL. If it comes back to you, let me know. We'll start with the cold tomatoes. *(Opens jar of tomatoes, puts one on spoon, moves it toward BOB's mouth.)*

BOB. Not tomatas! I *hate* 'em!

BILL. You'll hate 'em more when this is over.

BOB. No! Not yet!

BILL. Okay. *(Puts tomato back in jar.)* We'll do the Karo syrup first.

BOB. Yeah.

BILL. Open wide. *(BOB opens his mouth very wide, like a child; BILL fills teaspoon, gives it to BOB, who swallows.)* Okay, open up for number two.

BOB. *(Swallows it.)* Y'ain't givin' up on me Bill?

BILL. Down the hatch. *(BOB swallows.)* Now a tomato.

BOB. *(BILL puts a tomato on the spoon; holds it in front of BOB; BOB cringes, squirms.)* I'm sorry, Bill. Lettin' folks down is the story of my life. I'll never make this up to you.

BILL. You're not eatin' your tomato. *(BOB puts hand over his mouth; BILL holds BOB'S nose, throws in a tomato, BOB gags, spits it out; BILL takes handkerchief and, face to face, wipes off tomato; pause; their eyes meet; a tender moment; pause.).* Okay, let's get you up to bed. *(Replaces jars on shelf.)*

BOB. *(Suddenly with new conviction.)* Bill?

BILL. Yeah?

BOB. I'm gonna do whatever it takes to get sober — and stay that way.

BILL. *(Taking it in.)* I hear you, partner, loud 'n clear. C'mon. *(BILL slings BOB'S arm over his shoulder, his arm around his waist.)*

BOB. *(Remembering)* Socks.

BILL. Socks?

BOB. In my socks.

BILL. What's in your socks?

BOB. The goofballs.

BILL. The goofballs?

BOB. Upstairs, in my sock-drawer, in my socks.

(BILL laughs, as does BOB — and groans. BILL supporting him, BOB staggers to EXIT.)

Scene 14

AKRON, SAME TABLE, THREE DAYS LATER, THE DAY OF THE OPERATION, EARLY EVENING.

(ANNE sits at table. BILL stands, fidgetty, staring out at nothing. They are waiting for BOB, who is four hours late. Time hangs heavy. Apprehension is thick in the air.)

ANNE. *(Holding a battered old metal coffee pot.)* More coffee?

BILL. Any more coffee, I'll crawl right out of my skin.

ANNE. I keep seeing in my mind's eye the way he looked this morning, when we drove him to the hospital. The way his hands were shaking.

BILL. Yeah, I was worried too.

ANNE. Hands too shaky to grasp a steering wheel, and we placed a scalpel in those hands?

BILL. *(Trying to joke about it.)* Yeah, well, treating a drunk with the shakes is tricky: you've got to sedate 'em enough to kill the shakes, but stop before you kill the drunk.

ANNE. Bill! *(Recalling)* What was that you gave him in the parking lot?

BILL. What?

ANNE. *(Suspicious)* Bill?

BILL. *(Reluctantly)* Oh, well, I figured he needed a little fine tuning, that's all.

ANNE. *What* did you give him?

BILL. One more goofball and that last bottle of beer, and he seemed about right, didn't he? Perked right up, didn't he?

ANNE. I would not call it 'perked,' no.

BILL. He was walking straight — well, pretty straight — by the time he finally got to the main entrance.

ANNE. Not like he *can* walk. *(Pause)* And where is he now? When he called he said he'd be right home — it's been four hours! It'd be just like him to go out celebrating, and ruin it all.

BILL. No, I don't think that's it.

ANNE. You're such an optimist.

BILL. At my best, yes.

ANNE. Real moxie, you. All these years I've clung to my faith, clung to my Bible — sometimes literally — but I lost all hope for him. Doesn't take much anymore, to tip me over. Y'know, Bob courted me for many years, but I wouldn't marry him until he ceased drinking. And for a year he did. That's when we married. I did have hope, then.

BILL. And now?

ANNE. Perhaps. Those first two weeks after you arrived was the longest stretch he's been sober these twenty years. That's why I didn't want you to send him off to the convention. *You* know what it was like for me to sit here and wait, for those five days. So many nights I'd sit here, the children asleep, the house still as death but for the clock, ticking. Sitting with the feeling of hope and dread, when a car comes up, and then passes by?

BILL. I know all about dread.

ANNE. Do you know about waiting for someone?

BILL. To come home?

ANNE. To come alive. Waiting for someone else, someone you love, to come alive?

BILL. *(Taken aback.)* I…no, I can't say I do.

ANNE. And to be honest, Bill, I really don't think you *can* know. *(Considering)* But your wife probably could. Is she coming out here?

BILL. *(Dodging the question.)* I hope so.

ANNE. You've been apart for quite a long time now. I can't help wondering what she's thinking of all this.

BILL. Hard to tell.

ANNE. I think this is the time for her to come for a visit. Perhaps I'll write to her myself.

BILL. *(Squirming at this thought.)* Yeah, yeah —

(Sound of car in driveway, stops.)

ANNE. Hush! Listen.

(They strain to hear. Sound of CAR DOOR SLAMMING. LONG PAUSE.
BOB ENTERS, exhausted. Stands shyly before them, his summer straw hat in his hands.)

BOB. Don't worry, I'm okay.

ANNE. Thank God.

BOB. Patient's okay too.

ANNE. Where have you been?

BOB. Well…I'll tell you…a real strange thing…*(Pause; from his soul.)* I've been drivin' all over Akron…lookin' up every person I've harmed…Went to every one of our creditors, Annie, all the people I've been avoidin', some for years. I told 'em exactly what's been goin' on, expressed my wish to make amends. Even told Hubert, down at the mortgage bank — imagine that? *(ANNE is amazed.)* I've had enough. By tomorrow mornin' everybody in Akron'll know. But I told Bill I'd do whatever it takes, no matter what, 'n I guess this is it. Could be our ruin, Annie, but so be it. Sorry it took so long. Reckon it shows just how much harm I've done.

(Pause. ANNE, on verge of tears, looks to BILL, then down into lap.)

BOB. There's one more amends I have to make. *(He walks to table, bends down on one knee, offers her his hand; she takes it.)* Anne, I'm sorry. Sorry for all the pain I've caused you. From now on I'll let my actions speak for me, showin' you a man who is a husband, and a father, and even a surgeon, too.

(ANNE and BOB embrace, tenderly. Gently, she disengages. Slightly embarrassed by BILL seeing this moment.)

ANNE. *(Tearful)* Yes, well…I'd best get dinner. *(EXITS)*

BOB. *(Calling after.)* But if there's a single tomato involved, I'll scream! *(To BILL.)* Slimy red recalcitrant bastards.

(ANNE ENTERS, carrying a steaming pot of stew, puts it on table.)

ANNE. *(Holds out her hands for a 'Grace'.)* Shall we give thanks?

(They join hands and bow heads, for a silent 'Grace'. BILL and BOB glance furtively at each other, and then at ANNE who, with her eyes closed in prayer, doesn't notice, and raise their joined hands in triumph.)

Scene 15

(In spot one side of stage, LOIS sits at a kitchen table in Brooklyn, reading letter from BILL out loud.)

LOIS. "— and so, Lois, hard to believe it's two months since I moved in with Bob and Anne. Each morning we sit in silence, asking for guidance. Most nights Bob and I are up 'til two or three in the morning, drinking coffee, trying to develop our program. Bob says this could just be a fluke unless we prove it with others. So we're off to work on our first case — another surgeon! Remind me *never* to have my appendix out in Akron!"

(Light down on LOIS.
Light up on COCKTAIL BAR in Akron. Dance music. BILL and BOB stand at the bar; LLOYD, the surgeon, in a loud sports coat; MYRNA, a working class woman dressed provocatively, is exiting to get drinks; both she and LLOYD are tipsy.)

MYRNA. Wheee! *(Exits)*

LLOYD. Now listen, Bob — I'm on a roll here tonight, don't mess me up. This is not the place to talk.

BOB. The other night when we came by your house and told our stories, you said you'd make a surrender, and —

LLOYD. In front of my wife what the hell else would I say!

BOB. People at the hospital are talkin', Lloyd.

LLOYD. They talked about you too, Bob, drinking, and now they're talking about you sober — I don't give a good goddamn about any of it! Leave me alone.

(MYRNA RETURNS with drinks.)

BILL. We can't leave you alone, Lloyd.

LLOYD. *(Furious)* Hey buddy you don't know shit from Shinola about me! The last three days every time I turn around it's The Temperance Twins, selling salvation! I've half a mind to nail you, Mr. Bigshot Stockbroker —

(LLOYD pushes BILL, who pushes him back — into MYRNA — screaming and yelling; LLOYD swings at him; BILL swings back; MYRNA grabs LLOYD; BOB grabs BILL, holds him.)

LLOYD. Okay okay. *(Seems to calm down, takes his drink, puts a hand on BOB'S shoulder.)* Know what I think? *(Throws drink in BOB'S face.)* There's your drink! There you go. Drink up!

(BOB spits it out, wipes it off thoroughly. Lights down on Cocktail Lounge.
Lights up on Brooklyn.)

LOIS. *(Reading letter)*: "— so we ran into a slight snag with Lloyd. But we're learning — never try to work with drunks in bars. We've got a perfect prospect now, young fella named Eddie, he's connected to all the best circles in Akron, so if we get *him*, we're *in*! He, his wife Ruthie, and the two little kids...*(Amazed)* moved in with us? We tapered Eddie down with tomatoes, but then he tried to *commit suicide*. When we got him back he got angry at a tuna fish sandwich and threatened Anne with a knife. So we locked him up down in the coal cellar and started our treatment again. *(Astonished at the next sentence.)* I *do* wish you'd come here on your…*vacation*, darling. *(A beat; a 'look'.)* It must be hard for you alone to...manage the finances, but somehow I know that will all take care of itself."

(Lights down on Brooklyn. Spot up on BILL in Akron, reading letter from LOIS.)

BILL. "Dear Bill. I'm very disappointed you're not coming home. There are no finances to manage, and *nothing* will take care of itself! If you don't bring in some money soon, we'll lose Father's house. I'm still not clear what happened with the proxy fight. Anne wrote me, inviting me to come. I don't know whether to join you or not. I feel quite lonely, but *my life is here." (BILL EXITS.)*

(Lights up Akron; EDDIE and RUTHIE'S bedroom upstairs; after midnight; EDDIE, in undershirt, looking crazed and fierce, paces around his wife, RUTHIE, an attractive and intelligent young woman, wearing a nightgown. EDDIE is on a short fuse, stalking her. RUTHIE is scared, trying to back out the door, fearing that if she calls out he'll attack.)

EDDIE. *(Suspicious)* — and so, Ruthie, I was in the hospital, and you were at the Oxford Group meeting?

RUTHIE. Just like every Wednesday night for the past month, Eddie. There was nothing abnormal about —

EDDIE. I see. *(Pause)* And at the meeting, what exactly did you say?

RUTHIE. I told you, I made a surrender. *(Trying to slip out door.)* God it's hot! I think I'll just go down to the icebox and get a glass of milk.

EDDIE. Milk? Milk? You never drink...*milk. (Pause)* And what else did you tell them?

RUTHIE. *(Really scared.)* Nothing, Eddie. There's nothing to be suspicious about —

EDDIE. Did you talk about *me*?

(EDDIE throws her down on the bed, hand at her throat.)

RUTHIE. *(Gasping for air.)* No, I spoke about myself.

EDDIE. *(Furious)* Did you tell them about our *conjugal* life?

RUTHIE. Eddie, why are you so mad?

EDDIE. Mad?! You think I'm mad?! *(Strangling her; RUTHIE screams.)* Hunh? HUNH!

(Knock on door. EDDIE jumps off RUTHIE, puts finger to his lips, warning her not to tell.)

BOB. *(Asking through the shut door.)* Everything all right in there?

EDDIE. Yup.

BOB. Ruthie?

RUTHIE. Yes, fine...fine.

BOB. *(ENTERS with BILL and ANNE.)* Thought we heard a commotion up here.

EDDIE. Couldn't sleep.

BILL. *(Angry)* You sleep with your clothes on now Eddie?

EDDIE. Hardly sleeping at all. This treatment of yours is for shit.

BILL. *(Enraged)* Yeah well maybe it's just *you,* pal!

BOB. *(Taking charge.)* Look, Eddie, I think we'd best separate you and Ruthie tonight. You stay out in the garage. March.

(BOB starts to EXIT with EDDIE.)

EDDIE. *(To RUTHIE.):* I'm sorry.

(As BOB and EDDIE EXIT, BOB shoots a look of irritation at BILL.
BILL and ANNE go to RUTHIE.)

BILL. What happened, Ruthie?

(Pause. RUTHIE hangs her head, but says nothing.)

ANNE. Are you all right? *(No response.)* You can tell us, dear.

RUTHIE. I'd better check on the children.

(RUTHIE EXITS with ANNE, who also glares in irritation at BILL.
BOB RE-ENTERS.
PAUSE. A feeling of gloom and doom in the air.)

BOB. Y'know, this doesn't feel right.

BILL. Why the hell doesn't the guy get it?

BOB. He may be more than we can handle.

BILL. We've *got to* sell him on this! Damnit if we can get somebody like *him,* this thing'll take off!

BOB. *(Appalled)* Maybe the only way to sell this thing is to stop trying so hard to sell it.

BILL. *(Stung)* You sayin' *I'm* off, here? You sayin' there's something wrong with *me*?

BOB. No, no. *(Trying to be tactful.)* I'm sayin'...never-mind.

BILL. *(Lashing out at him.)* If I hadn't showed up you'd still be planted in your chair like a pumpkin, and —

BOB. I'm sayin'...we can't let what *we* want get in the way of reality anymore.

BILL. You mean what *I* want. *Me?* Right?

BOB. *(Losing it.)* Yeah, *you* — you and your goddamn ego the size of the Chrysler Building! *(Catching himself.)* Oh God...

BILL. *(This hits him hard; sinks down onto bed.):* Great. That's just great.

(BOB, ashamed of his outburst, tries to compose himself. RUTHIE and ANNE RE-ENTER.)

BOB. Ruthie, I'm sorry that we didn't understand earlier that we're putting you —

ANNE. Bob? *(He stops.)* Bill? This situation requires more than we can provide here. With Ruthie's permission I think you need to place a call to Ypsilanti.

BILL. What's Ypsilanti?

BOB. State Asylum. Michigan. *(To RUTHIE.)* Is that all right with you, Ruthie?

RUTHIE. I...I guess so. *(Thinking it over.)* I'll take the children to my parents' house in Anne Arbor. Thank you for trying.

(She and ANNE EXIT.)

BILL. *(Stunned, overwhelmed with despair, deflating.)* He could've killed her. What the hell do we think we're doing? This is not working.

BOB. It *is* working.

BILL. Yeah, sure.

BOB. Eddie's doin' us a favor.

BILL. Hunh?

BOB. He's keepin' *us* sober. Fella like Eddie could keep a whole army sober!

BILL. *(All doom and gloom.)* Terrific. Thank Eddie for me, willya?

(BILL trudges to EXIT.)

Scene 16

AKRON TRAIN STATION

(Sound of train easing in. BILL waits, his whole manner is depressed, gloomy. LOIS ENTERS, dressed for travel, wearing hat, carrying suitcase. Long look, and then they embrace.)

BILL. *(Trying to disguise his gloom.)* Great to see you baby.

LOIS. *(Notices)* And you.

BILL. I like your hat — is it new?

LOIS. Old, and mended.

BILL. I know the feelin'. You look terrific. I'm glad you've come.

LOIS. *(Coolly)* Shall we go?

BILL. *(Sensing something.)* What? What is it?

LOIS. We'll get to it.

BILL. No, no c'mon, what?

LOIS. Loesser's gave me the week off, but I don't know how long I'll be staying.

BILL. *(Startled)* What do you mean? What are you saying?

LOIS. *(Trying to put it delicately.)* On the train, I kept going over and over these things. I came here to see what was really happening, but also —

BILL. Hey I know how strange this must seem — even I have my doubts...

LOIS. Bill, what you're doing here — it sounds *completely insane.*

BILL. *(Pause)* I know. Remember that fella Eddie I wrote you about?

LOIS. Yes?

BILL. Sent him to a lunatic asylum. Split up the family — the whole nine yards.

LOIS. And so it's still just you and Bob?

BILL. *(Picks up suitcase.)* Let's go. They're dying to meet you.

LOIS. *(Not moving.)* And the proxy fight?

BILL. What *is* this?

LOIS. I need to be clear about these things.

BILL. *(A shrug.)* It's dead. I failed.

LOIS. I see. And you're still not about to come home?

BILL. I can't yet, no.

LOIS. You 'can't'? *(A beat.)* Bill, I've got some bad news. I wanted to tell you face to face, not in a letter. *(Pause;*

a bombshell.) Ebby's drinking again. He's been drunk for weeks.

BILL. What? *(Devastated, putting down suitcase.)* Ebby?

LOIS. I think we'd best go back home tomorrow. *(Pause)* Now take me to meet the Smiths.

(They EXIT, first LOIS, BILL stumbling after her.)

Scene 17

LIVING ROOM

(BOB and ANNE are waiting, nervously. LOIS ENTERS, followed by BILL, who is preoccupied and gloomy, carrying suitcase.)

ANNE. Lois?

LOIS. You must be Mrs. Smith.

ANNE. *(Takes her hand.)* So good to meet you.

LOIS. And you.

ANNE. This is my husband, Robert.

BOB. Call me Bob. Everybody else does. If I'm lucky.

LOIS. I appreciate your welcoming Bill into your home.

BOB. Pleasure's ours. *(Picking up BILL's gloom.)* Mostly. 'lo there, William.

(Pause.)

BILL. She wants me to come home.

(Long pause. A sense of doom hangs in the air. BOB and ANNE, embarrassed to witness this, exchange glances.)

ANNE. *(Gives him a nudge.)* Robert?

BOB. *(At first reluctantly, then with growing power.)* Yes, well. I don't mean to butt in...In my view, your husband is an unusual man.

LOIS. *(With irony.)* Yes, I know.

BOB. He's got real vision, rare to find. *(BILL groans in contempt.)* Not much patience, mind you, but a good deal 'a vision.

BILL. Thanks a million.

BOB. You're welcome. *(Back to LOIS.)* When I hit rock-bottom, he picked me up and walked me through to the other side. He *cared* for me. For all his talk, now that he's sober, I think you can believe him. *(Trying to lighten things.)* Y'see, he always wants too much, and has to settle for less; I always want too little, and have to settle for more. When he says something new could be happening here, I myself tend to give him the benefit of the doubt.

ANNE. I might add, Lois, that for a Vermont native to say such a thing — well, it's high praise.

LOIS. I appreciate your saying that, Bob. Very much. I signed on with him long before you did — *(Ironically; a wry first smile, to ANNE)* — and for reasons which, at this moment, are not crystal clear.

ANNE. Yes, dear, I know. I also know that the men are sober, thank the Lord. That is an actual fact. *(Pause)* You must be tired. *(Nudges BILL away from the suitcase, picks it up.)* Why don't we put you in your *own* room, overlooking the garden. *(BILL shows his surprise at this sleeping arrangement, as does BOB.)* It's quiet, and gets the morning sun.

LOIS. That's very kind of you. *(A look to BILL.)* I should think that would be best, for now.

(ANNE and BOB start off; LOIS goes to BILL, a private moment.)

LOIS. I'll stay out the week. That's all I can promise. I'll stay out the week.

Scene 18

LIVING ROOM; HOT WEATHER

(BILL is slumped deep into DR. BOB'S old easy chair, lying almost horizontally, totally motionless, battered hat covering his face. LOIS sits reading a magazine, restlessly. ANNE sits, knitting.
BOB ENTERS, in summer straw hat, carrying his doctor's bag.)

BOB. Good afternoon, ladies.

(Stares at BILL, then at ANNE, who indicates that BILL has not stirred. BOB slams his doctor's bag down on the table next to BILL — no reaction. Goes around table to BILL and, at ear-level, jingles pocket-change loudly — still no reaction.)

LOIS. *(Rising)* I need some fresh air. I'm going for a walk. *(Hesitates, then chances it.)* Bill? *(No response.) Bill! (Raises his hat, stares blankly at her, starts to lower hat again.)* Walk?

(Long pause; BILL shakes his head, lowers hat. LOIS starts to hurry out.)

ANNE. Do you want company? I'd be glad to —

LOIS. Thanks but no. I just need to clear my head *(EXITS)*

(Pause.)

BOB. You plannin' on gettin' outa that chair anytime soon, William?

BILL. *(Pause)* Maybe.

BOB. I haven't been able to get in my chair for two days now. *(No reponse.)* If you're thinkin' of tryin' to set a new world record, you should know I used to *live* in that chair. Lyin' in the exact same direction, right Annie?

ANNE. Head toward Mount Peace Cemetery.

BILL. *(Slowly rising.)* I'll go back upstairs to bed.

BOB. *(Cheerfully)* I've been thinkin', Bill, about where we've been goin' wrong? *(No response from BILL.)* We need to find ourselves a steady supply of more *reliable* alcoholics — ones already in the hospital. They always have a batch down at Akron City. What say, Bill?

BILL. *(Total gloom.)* Maybe it's finished...Maybe she's right...Time to go home.

BOB. You can't do that.

BILL. The hell I can't. I can be on the first train tomorrow headed for New York —

BOB. You're headed for a drink, Abercromb —

BILL. I told you — don't call me Abercrombie!

BOB. You're still headin' for a drink.

BILL. What do you know?

BOB. That I know. The old Bill, going under, would try to drink himself out of it —

BILL. But the new Bill, feeling like shit, has the great opportunity of going under sober. Hallelujah!

BOB. Who asked you how you feel?

BILL. That's the most bone-headed thing I —

BOB. Feelin's ain't facts. Just 'cause your ego's a little beat up doesn't mean the world's comin' to an end. Whoever said livin' sober would be easy?

BILL. I'm sick and tired of your two-bit Midwestern philosophy —

BOB. Yeah well that red-hot New York wit is wearin' a bit thin lately too.

BILL. Anne, this man is insufferable! Why'd you ever marry him?

(Pause)

ANNE. Insufferability was high on my list.

BOB. It's like the one about the policeman shinin' a light on a couple makin' love in the park? "It's all right, officer," the fella says, "we're married." "Sorry," says the cop, "I didn't know it was your wife." "Neither did I," says the fella, "'til you shined your light on us."

(Puzzled pause. Neither ANNE nor BILL sees the relevance of this.)

BILL. *(Exasperated)* What the hell is that supposed to mean?

BOB. It means that this treatment of ours can't rely on blinding flashes of light, it's about gettin' back to basics — the body, human nature — like the rest of medicine: step by step you try 'n put the pieces of the puzzle together, until one day the familiar's right there in front of your eyes. Get it?

(BILL just stares at him, not moving.)

BOB. *(Talking to BILL, while picking up phone and dialing.)* Yep, Akron City Hospital. I know the admitting nurse down there. Bet she's got a nice, neat, well-behaved drunk, just *dyin'* for what we got. *(Into phone, with bravado.)* Nurse Hall? Dr. Bob Smith here. Fella from New York and I have just found a cure for alcoholism, and we need — *(Pause)* That's right, a cure for alcoho — *(A beat.)* Matter 'a fact I *have* tried it on myself, and it works. *(Pause)* Why thank you, Nurse Hall. Y'got any drunks down there we can work on? *(Pause; repeating for BILL and ANNE'S benefit; delighted.)* He punched you in the eye? *(Pause; even more delighted.)* And you knocked him out! Nice goin', Hilda! *(Pause)* Say, what kind of bird is this egg when he's sober? *(Pause)* A grand chap. Lawyer! Wife's a peach, too. Dandy. My partner and I will be down there tomorrow. Thanks. Bye now. *(Hangs up.)* Hear that, Sir William? *(No response from BILL, who is slouching toward door; BOB shouts, like a command.) Sir William! (BILL stops, halfway turns.)* This one sounds perfect.

(BILL gives him a look, turns away.)

ANNE. May I make a suggestion?

(Both BILL and BOB turn to her.)

ANNE. Talk to his wife, first?

(BOB and BILL look at each other.)

Scene 19

THAT NIGHT. BEDROOM IN BOB'S HOUSE

(Sound of crickets. LOIS is packing. BILL is pacing. A silent, still night as the heat wave goes on. Significant emotional distance between then.)

BILL. You sure you're leaving.

LOIS. Yes.

BILL. You think this is crazy.

LOIS. *(Choosing her words carefully.)* I *think* I want you to come home.

BILL. Not sure?

LOIS. You've hardly talked to me for three days. You're in your own world.

BILL. If I go back to the city before we've got something that works, I'm dead.

LOIS. Is this working? *(Resumes packing.)*

(Pause)

BILL. The tide's gone out, and I'm staring at a lot of wreckage. And without booze, it's a helluva lot worse! I'm dying for a drink! Bob looks solid, but believe me, he could take a drink in a second. This thing has got to be greater than just him and me.

(Pause; she takes this in.)

LOIS. I see. Maybe your hope is here. But I'm trying to hold onto our life in New York.

BILL. I've crossed a line, but I don't know where the hell I'm going. Please, Lo, stay with me.

LOIS. Why should I?

BILL. From our first summer, we've always made these crossings together.

LOIS. No we have not.

BILL. What do you mean?

LOIS. Do you truly want to know?

BILL. Yes. *(LOIS doesn't answer; pause.)* I'm listening.

LOIS. *(A glance, then deciding to do it.)* Somewhere along the way, I found myself alone. Alone and helpless over you. I knew the terrible losses in your life. I thought I could make up for them; I found that I could not. And when you're alone, you have choices: stay, or leave; resentment, or understanding. These choices *must* be made. *(Pause)* I chose to stay, to try and find meaning. One day, I realized that my loneliness had turned to solitude. I may not have the life I imagined, but I'm learning to live the life I have. *(Emphasizing) I* have. Noticing things. Like someone else's child smiling up at me.

BILL. I know what that's like.

LOIS. Do you know what it's like for *me*? Have you ever really asked?

(Pause)

LOIS. I'm finding my own way — out of the whirlwind of you! And I'm not sure, even now, that you know what it's like when someone you love, night after night and then day after day isn't there, isn't really there.

BILL. *(Finally sensing it from her side.)* I've let you down so badly. I've missed you coming alive! *(Pause)* I'm so sorry.

(BILL goes to her and takes her hand; LOIS lets him, and for a moment starts to move toward him — but then she puts a hand on his chest, stopping him, and turns away.)

Scene 20

CITY HOSPITAL. A HOT NIGHT.

(BILLY DOTSON, a wiry little man with a southern accent, lies on a hospital bed.
In the hallway outside, HEN, his wife, a sassy, long-suffering woman with a southern accent, stands talking with BOB. BILL stands back, gloomy; he is reluctantly there.)

HEN. *(Fed up.)* This is the eighth time Billy's been in this hospital in the last six months. I've had it. I mean *I really have had it!* How much does this 'Program' of yours cost?

BOB. Nuthin'

HEN. You on the level?

BOB. We can't do it without your help.

HEN. I'll tell you somethin'. This time I did somethin' I never did before. I went to our pastor and I said, "You're not reachin' him. I'm goin' to find someone who can, if I have to search all of Akron." I *prayed* for that, 'n now you two show up! Well God must have some sense 'a humor!

BOB. Yes ma'am. But we're just tryin' to keep from takin' a drink ourselves.

HEN. Oh. Pardon my sayin' this, but that sounds a little bit *strange?* I mean I was prayin' for someone to help *him.*

BOB. *(At his wits end of how to deal with her, turning to BILL, gesturing him to try to help him out.)* Anything *you* want to throw in?

(BILL stares at him, slowly shakes his head 'No.')

BOB. *(Turning back to HEN.)* Please, ma'am? Please?

HEN. *(Considers this for a moment.)* Well okay then. I'll tell him you're here.

(She walks to BILLY'S bedside; he sits up, looking and feeling like shit.)

HEN. I've been talkin' to a couple of men about your drinkin'.

BILLY. I resent that. My wife talkin' to strangers.

HEN. Don't worry, they're drunks, just like you. One of 'em's a doctor.

BILLY. A drunk doctor. Well that's the cat's balls.

HEN. Shhh!

BILLY. Christ it's hot!

HEN. These two fellas want to come talk to you. They say it's gonna help *them* stay sober.

BILLY. Help *them*? That's rich. How much is this one gonna cost?

HEN. They won't take money. They're more than a little strange.

BILLY. No foolin'. Sure, tell 'em to come by sometime next week.

HEN. Un hunh. They're waitin' outside. *(BILLY is shocked; she EXITS; to BOB.)* Okay, go on in!

BOB. *(Hands her a note he has written.):* Here ma'am, take this. *(He escorts her out, talking to her; then turns to BILL.)* Ready? *(BILL pauses, then nods.)*

(BOB ENTERS, followed by a reluctant BILL, and go to either side of BILLY's bed.)

BOB. 'lo there. I'm Bob Smith and this is Bill Wilson.

BILLY. Which one a you is the drunk doctor?

BOB. That'd be me. And my friend Bill here is a drunk stockbroker.

BILLY. Oh boy! *(Pause)* I'm Bill Dotson. They call me Billy.

BOB. Heard you gave Nurse Hall a black eye the other night.

BILLY. So they say. Don't recollect the incident myse'f.

BOB. We drunks do terrible things in blackouts, right Bill?

BILL. *(Eyes him; reluctantly.)* One morning I woke up in a jail cell not knowing which *country* I was in. Didn't look like America. I guessed Canada. Turned out to be Cuba.

BILLY. Yeah I know all about that. Not that I ever been in Cuba…*(Considers this.)* Don't *think* I have, anyway.

BOB. I got to hidin' bottles from the wife, and then couldn't find em. Over doorjambs… *(Gestures to BILL to 'come on, get with it'.)*

BILL. Down the clothes chute…

BOB. In the coal bin...

BILL. Ash container of the furnace...

BOB. Water tank of the toilet... *(They both look at BILLY.)*

BILLY. *(Hesitates, then smiles, joining in, loudly.)* Dog house!

(They exchange smiles; a first moment of real contact.)

BOB. I myself got to walkin' around with ten 4-ounce bottles stuffed in my socks. But then one day the wife and kids went to the pictures t'see *Tugboat Annie*, and Wallace Beery used the same hidin' place. They all came home and *dove* for my socks! *(Pause; suddenly sombre.)* It was humiliatin'.

BILLY. No foolin'. *(Sighs)* I been in here so many times, shackled t'the bed for near two, three days 'fore I even knew where I was. *(Pause)* I reckon it's time, in this pitiful life, to piss on the fire and call in the dogs. *(Closes eyes, in depths of self-pity and despair.)*

(BOB and BILL look at each other. BILL won't join in yet.)

BOB. How'd you get to this point, Billy?

BILLY. Think I know? I'm from a good farm family, Carlyle County, Kentucky. One day when I was eight I was he'pin the hired hands clear out the barn. I started in on some hard cider from a barrel, passed out, and was carried into the house. Next day, I feel like shit — and what do I do?

BOB. Make a beeline for that barrel in the barn —

BILLY. It was *love*! So I joined the United States Army,

and got *paid* to drink. Got married. Nice house. Nice kids. Akron Law School, Akron City Council. *(Pause)* But the last few years, it's gone all to hell. *(Disgusted with himself.)* Ah t'hell with it.

BOB. Bill?

BILL. *(Assesses BILLY, and their chances with him.)* Maybe.

BOB. Good. *(Pulls up a chair, sits. To BILLY.)* Son, we feel we've been given a gift — the gift of sobriety — and it's a strange sort of gift, 'cuz the only way we get to keep it is to pass it on.

BILLY. Nobody's givin' me any gifts lately.

BOB. Billy, you've got a disease.

BILLY. A *disease?*

BOB. Called alcoholism.

BILLY. You're shittin' me.

BOB. An *incurable disease.*

BILLY. Jesus Christ!

BOB. That's right.

BILLY. How'd I get it?

BOB. We all may've been born with it.

BILLY. Will you tell that to the wife?

BOB. Be glad to. We think there may be a treatment. We think we can stay sober by takin' it to somebody else that needs it, and *wants* it. Now if you don't want it, say no, and we'll be goin'.

BILLY. Yeah I guess I'd like to quit for — let's see — two, three, maybe five months —'til I get things straightened out. *(BILL and BOB laugh.)* What's so funny about that?

BILL. Whether you quit for five days, five months, or five years, if you start again you'll end up right back here, tied down six ways from Sunday.

BOB. Now listen. Can you walk out of this hospital and never take another drink.

BILLY. *(Astonished, irritated.) Never?* What kinda question is that? I thought you —

BILL. *(Realizing)* Forget 'never'. Even we can't promise that anymore. Can you just make it through today?

BILLY. Today? I can't even get outa this bed today! Y'don't understand — I'm scared to leave this hospital at all.

BILL. We *do* understand that, friend. But is there anything outside of yourself you can rely on, or believe in?

BILLY. You don't have to sell me religion — I used to be the Deacon of our church, taught Sunday School for years. *(The memory of it hurts.)* Prayer don't work. I still believe in God, but I reckon God stopped believin' in me.

BOB. I doubt that, son.

BILLY. *You* licked this thing — how'd *you* do it?

BILL. *(Excited, suddenly again 'the preacher'.)* Y'see we've chiseled this thing down, and what we've found, right at the heart of it all, is this: you have to make a —

BOB. Hold on, partner!

BILL. He asked me, and I'm telling —

BOB. — *tellin'* him, I know.

BILL. *(Long moment.)* Yeah.

BOB. What my partner was about to say, Billy, is that we're no better than you, and no worse — just maybe a little farther along. We're just two bozos on a bus, makin' room for a third. We'll try to help you find your way.

BILL. And that's a promise.

BILLY. *(Touched)* Well thank you kindly, for that.

BOB. Billy, are you willin' to ask for help, and let go of booze entirely?

BILLY. *Entirely*?

BOB. And ask for help.

BILLY. *Entirely?*

BOB. *(Realizing he's blundered.)* Hang on, I…I didn't mean that, I —.

BILLY. But that's what you said. *(As a lawyer.)* That was your *statement*. Right?

BILL. *(Coming to BOB'S rescue.)* Hold it. Maybe we we're puttin' the cart before...Let's try it again. *(Eye to eye, really with him.)* Can you just ask for help?

(Long pause, as BILLY takes this in.)

BILLY. No. Can't say I'd do *that*, no.

BOB. But you said —

BILLY. No!

BOB. *(Disappointed)* Uh, well…sounds like y'need to think on it.

BILLY. *(Angrily)* No I do *not* need to think on it. Leave me alone! Don't waste your time on me!

(Lies back on bed, pulls sheet up to his chin, closes eyes.)

BOB. Okay. Let's go.

(BOB, discouraged, starts to leave the room; BILL also takes a couple of steps, but then stops BOB from leaving, brings him back to BILLY'S bedside. They stand side by side, looking down at BILLY.)

BILL. Billy?

(BILLY opens his eyes, and for a brief moment looks at them

standing there together; BILL holds BILLY'S gaze, then looks at BOB, then back at BILLY.)

BILL. *(Firmly; echoing what EBBY said to him in Town's.)* We'll be back tomorrow.

(BILL turns, walks away; BOB follows, out into the hospital corridor; BILLY watches them go.)

BOB. What was that all about?
BILL. Didn't you *feel* it?
BOB. Feel *what*?
BILL. The three of us, held together just for a moment, like…like three birds held, still, in a pocket of the wind!
BOB. *(Big smile; his partner is "back".)*: Fireworks and magic, eh Abercrombie? *(Laughs)*
BILL. *(Laughs; with affection.)* Yeah, Smithy. *(Pause)* Thanks.
BOB. *(Softly)* Yeah. *(They EXIT.)*

(NOTE: BILLY lying in bed stays onstage, in dim light, right through until epilogue.)

Scene 21

LATER THAT SAME EVENING. LIVING ROOM AT ARDMORE AVENUE. THREE CHAIRS — BOB'S CHAIR AND TWO OTHERS.

(LOIS is standing, ANNE sitting. They are dressed for another heat-wave evening. Coffee pot and cups on table.

There is still distance between them, reflected in the pauses, as they try to connect.)

LOIS. Are they always out this late?

ANNE. These days, yes. I've never seen two men so absorbed. *(Awkward pause; LOIS fidgets; ANNE brings her a cup of coffee.)* I'm so glad you stayed, Lois. *(ANNE sits again.)* At times like this, do you start to worry?

LOIS. Yes, I do. *(Discovering it.)* But seeing him here, with Bob, it seems that something new is taking hold It's rather shocking, actually.

ANNE. To hear you say that, well, it's a real treasure. It helps me very much.

LOIS. That's good. I'm glad.

(Pause)

ANNE. So many nights, I'd sit here alone, the main thing in my mind being whether or not to leave him.

LOIS. *(A question for herself as well.)* Why have *you* stayed?

ANNE. I loved the man I used to know. And I couldn't bear to think of him alone. Does that sound cowardly?

LOIS. Hardly. There's virtue in staying, too.

ANNE. There is, yes. *(Pause, then risking it.)* It used to be hardly a day would go by without my being angry at Bob. And then one evening when Bill and I were here waiting for him, I felt like I saw Bob's sickness ever so clearly — from close up and far away both — and I saw two ordinary people caught up in something terrible, yes, but nobody's fault, really. I let go! It helped me to be more forgiving.

LOIS. I wish I had your generosity. Sometimes I'm afraid that my anger's all that's kept me going.

ANNE. I don't see you so much as angry, dear, as spunky.

LOIS. *(Surprised)* Really?

ANNE. Yes. You're a strong person, when it comes to something you believe in.

LOIS. Yes, I suppose.

(Doorbell)

HEN. *(Offstage):* Hello?

ANNE. Come in?

HEN. *(ENTERING.):* Hello. I'm Hen, Billy Dotson's wife? *(No recognition of this.)* Are you Mrs. Smith?

ANNE. Yes. *(Pause)* This is Lois Wilson, from New York City.

HEN. Pleased to meet you.

LOIS. And you.

(Awkward pause.)

HEN. I was *told* to come over here.

ANNE. *(Surprised by this; a look to LOIS.) Who* told you, dear?

HEN. Dr. Smith. He's workin' on my husband tonight and he told me to come over here, but I said I was puttin' up peaches — at night, in this heat, boilin' peaches! — and he says to me: "Hen, what's more important, the peaches or your husband?" — and I had to say, "The peaches."

(All laugh; HEN'S laughter is frantic; they notice.)

ANNE. Sit, Hen, will you?

(HEN sits between them, agitated, ready to explode; pause.)

ANNE. Is everything all right?

HEN. Yes, yes…no. *(Bursting out with it, tearful.)* I hate him! I feel such hatred! Isn't that a terrible thing to say?

ANNE. No, dear. I'm sure it's merely the truth.

HEN. Truth is, I hate myself. It's like a poison in me. *(Pause)* Is this deranged?

LOIS. No, not at all.

HEN. It's a nightmare! *(Ashamed)* I can barely show my face in public.

LOIS. *(Touched)* There's no need to feel so apart.

HEN. How do you mean?

LOIS. *(Struggling to admit it.)* That's my situation too.

HEN. *(Startled)* You?

LOIS. Yes.

ANNE. And mine.

HEN. *Truly?*

ANNE. Yes, it is.

(Note: Light now is a glowing gold spot, as in BILL and BOB meeting scene.
Long pause. A real sense of connection between them.)

ANNE. Do you know, this is the first time, in all these years, that someone has sat with me in this room, in this way.

LOIS. *(Sensing the 'miracle' of it.)* Yes, it's quite an

adventure, isn't it? *(Putting her hand on HEN'S.)* Tell us more, Hen. We want to hear.

HEN. Truly? *(Looks first to LOIS, then to ANNE.)*

LOIS. Yes.

ANNE. Yes.

HEN. Thank you kindly. *(Pause)* The final straw was last week. My brother was gettin' married for the second time, small weddin', just family? So there we all are, dressed fit to kill, but my brother can't marry Wife Number Two, 'cause this idiot lawyer husband of mine hadn't gotten around to filin' the papers to divorce him from Wife Number One!

(A beat. All break out laughing.

BILL and BOB ENTER. Both are quiet, sobered by their work with BILLY.

Seeing the men come in, LOIS stands up and signals the women to stop laughing, but when they look at how serious the men look, they can't help themselves from bursting out laughing again. The men notice, and smile.)

BILL. Sorry we're so late. Bob and I —

LOIS. *(For the first time since she's arrived, warmly.)* It's good you were. Bill, dear?

(Holds out her hand; he comes to her, a kiss on the cheek, stand together arm in arm.)

HEN. *(Anxious)* Doc, how's my husband?

BOB. Dunno. He's a tough egg to crack.

HEN. Tell me the truth.

BOB. 'fraid it's not in our hands, now.

(BOB stands next to ANNE.
LONG SILENCE. GLOWING GOLD SPOT. A strange stillness falls over them. The sense is of a small close group of people, waiting. A vigil.
In dim spot, BILLY on the hospital bed.)

ANNE. When I was a girl, I was told that this kind of silence, at this time of night, meant there were angels passing, overhead. *(Pause; to HEN.)* Hen, dear, you stay here tonight, with us.

(HEN hesitates, then nods.
In synchrony, spot on BILLY and light on the others fade.)

Scene 22

THE NEXT MORNING. CITY HOSPITAL.

(BILLY is asleep on his hospital bed, peaceful. BILL and BOB ENTER. They put the back of the bed up, awakening BILLY. He is startled, not aware of where he is.)

BOB. Hey wake up, Billy. How'd ya sleep?

BILLY. Oh. You? Didn't think I slept a wink, but I guess I did.

BILL. So, Billy, what's it to be?

BILLY. *(Waking up, clearing the cobwebs.)* Well, I'll tell you. Lemmie see now. Yeah. Well after you boys left last night, I couldn't sleep. I kept thinking what liquor had done to me and my family...*(Fierce self-loathing.)* Scum. I'm scum. *(A challenge to them.)* You know what that feels like?

BILL. *(A glance a BOB.)* Yes, we do.

BOB. We sure do.

BILLY. I'd got ahold of somethin' I couldn't handle by myse'f. I *wanted* to ask for help like you said I had to, but the truth is...*I could not, no.*

(BILL and BOB look at each other in dismay and disbelief; BILL gets up.)

BILLY. Say hold on, hold on. I ain't finished yet. *(They wait.)* Would you boys mind if I got up, and we all set down together? Y'know, like on the same level?

BILL. 'Course not, Billy.

(BILLY tries to get up out of the bed, but can't — tumbles over on bed again, a pitiful sight.
BILL and BOB rush to him, help him up to his feet. They let go, he starts to fall, they grab him.)

BILLY. Christ I'm weak! Bring on the tomatoes!

(With painful slowness, they carry him to THREE CHAIRS downstage — same location as in BILL and BOB'S first meeting. What follows should echo that scene in many different ways — lighting, etc. BILLY sits in the middle chair, BILL and BOB on either side.)

BILLY. Thank y'kindly. So there I was, stuck for the longest time. But then, I recalled you two when you came back into my room last night. You two standin' there together, like you saw somethin' in me. And it's like when you pass a good card game 'n want in? Well boys, I wanted in.

BILL. Exactly.

BOB. Keep firin' Billy.

BILLY. An' I felt I'd give anything to be there with you, an' almost in spite of myse'f I found myse'f sayin', out loud, "If they can do it, I can do it; if they can do it, I can do it" — over and over again — and then I felt somethin' break free.

(A look to them, they show that they understand this, deeply.)

BOB. Yes.

(He looks at BILL; a moment, with a sense of awe.)

BILL. (Quietly): Yes.

(Note: light now is a glowing gold spot in the dark, as in BILL and BOB meeting scene. The three men sit on the edges of their chairs, leaning over and in toward each other, totally absorbed in talking and listening, attending and responding. Their hands and faces reveal their intensity, excitement, and power. The "feel" is of a tremendous sense of shared "spirit." BILLY has become the center of the three of them, sitting up straighter in his chair, speaking more and more confidently and forcefully. As he tells his story, the truth of it and their listening to it empowers him.)

BILLY. Well, all at once I knew I *could.* Things came clear, like a breeze was blowin' — not really in me or outside me, but all-around and in-between, like on a farm on a summer's day you can actually *see* the breeze, rufflin' the wheat! Y'ever seen that?

BOB. Beautiful sight!

BILLY. Beautiful!

BILL. *(With absolute conviction.)* Bob, *this is it.*

(BOB nods.)

BOB. *(To BILLY, wanting to be sure.):* So are you willin' to join us, Billy, and ask for help?

(Pause)

BILLY. *(Soberly)* Yes, friends, I am.

BLACKOUT

EPILOGUE

(As in PROLOGUE: stage black except, standing on opposite sides, BILL and BOB in two spots. They do not look at each other during this, but talk to audience.)

BILL. — and so Dr. Bob and I walked out of Billy D's room and one of us turned to the other and said, "Now we've got three members, that makes us a group." Billy D. left that hospital a free man, and we three went out looking for just one more, to pass it on —

BOB. — to pass it on. Y'know, even now I still think I could probably knock off a couple 'a scotches, but then I say to myself, 'Better get back on the job, big boy, better go see some of the drunks on the ward. "Giving of ourselves" — our own effort, strength, and time — that's what Bill learned in New York City, and I learned from Bill. Takes *practice,* y'know, to learn that spirit of service. *(Pause)* For you newcomers, I've got a few suggestions: take the cotton outa your ears and put it in your mouth; just sit, and listen. Do what each of us does: don't drink, ask for help, and go to meetin's. *(Pause; on verge of tears.)* Y'know, every time I'm at a meetin', I'm brought back to that first meetin', when Bill W. came into my life. Bill's a man I came to think of as a brother, and, strange, but all evenin' long he's been very much on my mind. And I reckon that for each of you it's the same — every meetin's like the first, an act of faith, drawin' us together, through that invisible thread that connects us — *(Pause, as he looks around the audience,) — all. (Pause)* Like to end our meetin' with a moment of silence. *(Bows head.)*

BILL. Let me close with a word about Dr. Bob. One

Sunday in November 1950 I traveled again to Akron, to ask Bob whether he and I should step down and turn over the governing of the fellowship to its members — a radical idea at the time. Bob was in terrible shape, deathly ill, but after careful thought he said, "Well, Sir William, it has to be AA's decision, not yours or mine. It's fine with me." *(Pause)* A few hours later I took my leave of Dr. Bob, knowing that the following week he was to undergo a very serious operation. Neither of us dared to say what was in our hearts. I went down the steps and then turned to look back. Bob stood in the doorway, tall and upright as ever. Some color had come back into his cheeks, he was carefully dressed in a light brown suit. This was my partner, the man with whom I never had a hard word. And then that wonderful smile lit up his face, and he said: *(Pause, on the verge of tears.)* "Remember, Bill, let's not louse this thing up. Let's keep it simple." *(Pause; difficulty speaking.)* That...that was the last time I ever saw him. *(Pause)* Like to end our meetin' with a moment of silence.

(Bows head.
This shared "moment of silence" lasts from 10 to 20 seconds. Then, together, spots on both men slowly fade to BLACK.)

NOTES

Page numbers, followed by indication of quotes taken from:

Alcoholics Anonymous (AA), Third Edition (1976), copyright 1939, 1955, 1976, by Alcoholics Anonymous World Services, Inc., NY.

Dr. Bob and the Good Oldtimers (DB), copyright 1980 by Alcoholics Anonymous World Services, Inc, NY.

"Pass It On", the story of Bill Wilson and how the A.A. message reached the world (PIO), copyright 1984 by Alcoholics Anonymous World Service Inc., NY.

Page 8: "Nobody but an Australian…boomerang." PIO p.29
Page 8: "when I was free…doors of a church again." DB p.229
Page 14: "work the harvest…for that little." DB p.229
Page 21: "All I ever wanted…and to tap dance." DB p.127
Page 27: "I'll do anything, anything at all!" PIO p.120
Page 28: "a free man." PIO p.121
Page 28: "Whatever you've got…had you." PIO p.123
Page 33: "on a twin-engine…One man." PIO p.131
Page 37: "Well, you good…secret drinker and I can't stop." DB p.58
Page 37: "Do you want us to pray for you?" p.58
Page 41: "My name's Bill…New York." PIO p.60
Page 41: "Oh my…Heaven." PIO p.60
Page 45: "The strange barrier…universe." PIO p.56
Page 48: "need another drunk…he needs." PIO p.136Page

Page 57: "I'm gonna do…and stay that way." DB p.74
Page 74: "shining…light on us." DB p.228
Page 75: "Fella from…cure for alcoholism." PIO p.152
Page 75: "What kind of bird…sober." DB p. 84
Page 78: "You're not reaching…Akron." DB p.83
Page 82: "we think we can…someone who does." AA p.186
Page 82: "if you start…tied down." AA page 187
Page 83: "Can you…drink?" AA page 186
Page 92: "If they can…I can do it." AA p.189
Page 94-95: "Let me close…ever saw him." DB p. 343

PROPERTY PLOT

6 chairs

Piano

One moveable bar (with shelves on one side—serves as bar, and hotel counter, and kitchen shelves in Akron house)

Kitchen table for Bill's house (serves as bar table etc.)

Small table with radio on it for Bob's house

Bed, which serves as hospital bed and as bedroom bed

Phone for Bob's house, and hotel phones

All other props are indicated in each scene

GROUND PLAN

The play is written to be done without a standard fixed set. The "setting" for each scene is suggested by simple props, chairs, tables, beds, etc. This design will allow the fluidity of staging that the play requires.

The Clean House

By Sarah Ruhl

2005 Pulitzer Prize Finalist

This extraordinary new play by an exciting new voice in the American drama was runner-up for the Pulitzer Prize. The play takes place in what the author describes as "metaphysical Connecticut", mostly in the home of a married couple who are both doctors. They have hired a housekeeper named Matilde, an aspiring comedian from Brazil who's more interested in coming up with the perfect joke than in house-cleaning. Lane, the lady of the house, has an eccentric sister named Virginia who's just nuts about house-cleaning. She and Matilde become fast friends, and Virginia takes over the cleaning while Matilde works on her jokes. Trouble comes when Lane's husband Charles reveals that he has found his soul mate, or "bashert" in a cancer patient named Anna, on whom he has operated. The actors who play Charles and Anna also play Matilde's parents in a series of dream-like memories, as we learn the story about how they literally killed each other with laughter, giving new meaning to the phrase, "I almost died laughing." This theatrical and wildly funny play is a whimsical and poignant look at class, comedy and the true nature of love. 1m, 4f (#6266)

"Fresh, funny ... a memorable play, imbued with a somehow comforting philosophy: that the messes and disappointments of life are as much a part of its beauty as romantic love and chocolate ice cream, and a perfect punch line can be as sublime as the most wrenchingly lovely aria." — *NY Times*